THE FLAMING TRAP

THE FLAMING TRAP

LEE RODDY

BETHANY HOUSE PUBLISHERS
MINNEAPOLIS, MINNESOTA 55438

Published by Bethany House Publishers
A Ministry of Bethany Fellowship, Inc.
6820 Auto Club Road, Minneapolis, Minnesota 55438

Printed in the United States of America

Library of Congress Cataloging-in-Publication Data

Roddy, Lee, 1921–
    The flaming trap / Lee Roddy.
        p.   cm. — (An American adventure ; bk. 5)

    Summary: Returning to the Ozark Mountains to visit their grandmothers, Hildy and Ruby encounter old mountain hatreds, danger, and God's marvelous forgiveness.
        [1. Ozark Mountains—Fiction. 2. Adventure and adventurers—Fiction. 3. Christian life—Fiction.]
    I. Title. II. Series: Roddy, Lee, 1921– American adventure ; bk. 5.
PZ7.R6F1   1990
[Fic.]—dc20   90–43546
ISBN 1–55661–095–5   CIP
                                                                          AC

To Norman and Virginia Rohrer
for opening the first door
to my writing career
in this field

AN
AMERICAN ADVENTURE
SERIES

LEE RODDY is a bestselling author and motivational speaker. Many of his more than 50 books, such as *Grizzly Adams*, *Jesus*, *The Lincoln Conspiracy*, the *D. J. Dillon Adventure Series*, and the *Ladd Family Adventures* have been bestsellers, television programs, book club selections or have received special recognition. All of his books support traditional moral, spiritual, and family values.

CONTENTS

CHAPTER
ONE

A SHADOW FROM THE PAST

Hildy Corrigan's heart began to beat faster. *I think somebody's following me!* she thought as she walked barefooted under the next-to-last streetlight near the end of the boardwalk. Beyond the final light there was a quarter-mile stretch of coal-black night where her father and cousin waited.

It's a man's footsteps, the twelve-year-old girl decided, listening hard to the sounds behind her. *When I come to the edge of town, and there's no light—*

She shook off the thought and glanced back again. She caught a brief glimpse of a man's shadowy figure about a block behind her. She couldn't see his face, because he quickly stepped into the deeper shadows under the sycamore and Dutch elm trees.

Hildy walked on, swallowing hard as she heard the stealthy footfalls behind her again. They were not in a hurry, but they were purposeful and steady. It had been that way from the moment she left Matthew Farnham's mansion after being inter-

viewed for a part-time job of helping his handicapped wife with
their small children.

Still listening anxiously to the footsteps behind her, Hildy
suddenly tensed. *I think he's walking faster!* She fought an urgent
feeling to pick up the hem of her ankle-length dress and start
running. Instead, she decided, *I'll cross the street and see if he
follows.*

She cut across the deserted street at the edge of the small
California ranching community of Lone River. Every step took
her away from the comfort of the next-to-last streetlight. Her
shadow grew longer, showing her slender body in the simple
dress and her waist-length braids.

"He's also crossing, so he *is* following me!" the words escaped her mouth, which was becoming increasingly dry with
fear. "Whoever it is obviously doesn't want me to see him. But
who is he? Why's he following me?" she whispered.

She was tempted to look back again while her pursuer was
visible under the streetlight. But she resisted doing that, because
she didn't want him to know she was afraid.

She thought of running up and knocking on one of the quiet
houses where electric lights burned. But what could she say?
Call the police. A man's following me?

Hildy knew that even if the town's one policeman questioned
her follower, he would deny that he meant any harm.

But what'll I do? she asked herself as she approached the last
streetlight. Beyond that, the totally black September night
stretched menacingly ahead.

She tried to slow her speeding heart by yielding to a com-
promise. *When I get to the city limits, I'll run to Dad and Ruby,* she
decided. *It's only a quarter mile or so. And whoever's following me
won't hear my bare feet on the dirt road!*

She forced herself to walk steadily, without seeming to hurry.
Still, she strained to hear her pursuer's footfalls above the crickets singing in the tall grass across the barbed-wire fence. The
stealthy sound of leather boot heels on the boardwalk continued
behind her.

Her blue eyes probed the early September night—the final

streetlight just ahead. The boardwalk ended there and so did the light. Only country darkness stretched ahead. There was no house for a quarter-mile. She could barely make out the light from the first isolated ranch house where her father and cousin were waiting. A lot could happen in the dense darkness between the last streetlight and that house.

Hildy made a sudden decision. *I've got to see who's following me!*

That entailed a certain risk, because she'd have to stop and wait until whoever was behind her passed under the last streetlight, and that would put him closer. Whoever was following would not be able to see Hildy in the darkness, but she would be able to see him as he passed under the streetlight. And, she reasoned, she was barefooted, and if necessary, could run faster than a man in heavy boots.

Fighting her rising fear, Hildy left the boardwalk and stepped onto the unpaved country road. Her bare feet made no sound in the dust as she moved toward a giant sycamore tree.

As the night wrapped her in total darkness, she made out the dark bulk of the sycamore's spreading crown against the star-flecked night sky. She approached the tree cautiously, feeling her way along the trunk.

Satisfied, she pressed herself flat against it and tried to still her thudding heart and irregular breathing. Cautiously, she peered back down the deserted street toward the streetlight. Except for the crickets and the approaching footsteps, there was total silence.

No cars or buggies were about. The Depression of 1934 still lay heavily on the small California ranching community. Few people went anywhere unless it was absolutely necessary.

A gentle breeze started up, bringing the faintest hint of coming autumn after a hot summer. The wind rustled the sycamore's leaves over Hildy's head, making a spooky sound, like a whispered warning for the lone girl not to linger. But she stayed, ready to break into a flat-out run toward her father and cousin.

Hildy strained to see a man's heavy boot step into the glow of the streetlight. Then she saw the pant leg of faded work overalls, the second booted foot, and finally the whole person came into view.

Oh! She instinctively jerked her head back against the tree trunk. *It can't be!* She closed her eyes tightly, as though to block out the sight, but the image burned brightly in her mind.

I've got to be sure! she told herself, opening her eyes and leaning forward just enough for another quick glance back. The white reflector on the streetlight swayed slightly as the wind touched the wires. The man didn't linger where he could be seen but stepped off the boardwalk into the silent dust, away from the light.

But the second glance had been enough for Hildy. *It's him!* she told herself in disbelief. *It's Vester Hardesty!*

The heavyset man with the pockmarked face and reddish beard wore the same patched overalls, faded blue denim shirt, and black slouch hat that he'd worn when he kidnapped Hildy and her cousin several weeks before in Illinois. The girls escaped, and the police apprehended Vester, but obviously they hadn't held him.

I've got to get away—fast! Hildy grabbed her long skirt and yanked the hem up over her knees.

She fled down the country road on silent bare feet, grateful that she did not hear the thud of heavy boots chasing after her. She didn't dare look back, but ran flat out, her long brown braids flying almost straight out behind her.

"I'm going to make it!" she panted aloud, almost sobbing with relief as she turned into the short dirt driveway of a small ranch house. She dashed around the side, too breathless to speak to the friendly old dog that barked an alarm.

Hildy raced past her father's newly acquired Rickenbacker straight-eight sedan, heading for the detached frame garage. A single electric light bulb, swinging gently from its long twisted cord, showed her father with his head under the right side hood of a boxy, 1929 two-door Chevrolet sedan.

Hildy dashed onto the dirt floor of the garage with its strong smell of grease and oil. She slid to a stop, glanced back in satisfaction and sighed with relief.

Her thirteen-year-old cousin stuck her head out of the right front passenger's window. "Hildy!" Ruby Konning exclaimed in her Ozark accent. "Ye look like ye seen a haint!" Ruby had ridden into town with her cousin and uncle because she planned to spend the night with Hildy and her family.

"It's him!" Hildy exclaimed, trying to catch her breath. She turned, panting, and pointed the way she'd come. "He's here!"

Hildy's father straightened up. His blue eyes were bloodshot from weariness as he wiped his greasy hands on an oil-stained rag. "Who's here?" he demanded, peering past his daughter into the darkness. "What're you talking about?"

"Vester!" Hildy cried, trying to stop a shiver that rippled over her shoulders and down her bare arms. "I saw him, plain as day! He followed me from Mr. Farnham's!"

"Vester Hardesty?" Ruby echoed, alarm in her voice. She jerked open the door of the sedan and slid her feet to the garage floor. She was shoeless and wore her usual tomboy clothing of blue overalls and work shirt. Ruby was an inch taller than Hildy and had blonde hair cut in a short, boyish style. "Y'all are a'tryin' to josh us, ain't ye, Hildy?"

Hildy shook her head so hard her waist-length braids flopped wildly about. "I'm telling you the gospel truth! He must have been waiting for me to leave Mr. Farnham's, because I heard him following me almost at once!"

Hildy quickly explained what had happened, and her father promptly drove the girls back to where Hildy had seen the man.

Hildy leaned back in the seat with a heavy sigh. "He's gone! But I tell you, it was Vester!"

Her cousin reached out a sturdy hand and patted Hildy's arm reassuringly. "We believe ye, don't we, Uncle Joe?"

Hildy's father nodded, his wide-brimmed cowboy hat bobbing in the faint light from the dashboard. "We do, Hildy. But what puzzles me is why he'd show up here and now. And how did he know to watch for you to come out of Matthew Farnham's place tonight?"

Hildy's heart had slowed to a near normal beat, but her mind was still racing. "I don't know! I don't even know how he found us here in California! But he didn't come nearly two thousand miles for no reason!"

"Yo're right!" Ruby declared. "An' ye know why! Yore o'nery old grandma sent him, jist like she done when we ran away in June!"

Hildy shook her head so hard one of her braids slapped across her cousin's bare arm. "Granny wouldn't send him clear to California for us! Vester must be doing it on his own—maybe because the police caught him in Illinois after he kidnapped us and we escaped!"

Ruby shuddered, her hazel eyes opening wide. "I 'member that! I bet he was mad enough to spit nails when we'uns got away! But I'm plumb certain that yore Granny sent him to bring us back."

Hildy was doubtful. "I don't think so. But maybe your grand-mother sent him to find you! I mean, the way we took off from the Ozarks without even telling her—"

Ruby interrupted, swiveling in the seat to face Hildy. "No, that ain't it. Muh grandma don't keer a kettle o' beans what happens to me. But yore granny'd give her eyeteeth to have ye back thar with her."

Joe Corrigan turned the long car around at an intersection and headed into the country. "Well, whatever his reason, I don't like having him around. He's certainly up to no good."

Ruby exclaimed, "Yo're plumb right! I'm certain that Hildy's granny done set him on us again—jist like she done last June!" Ruby added anxiously, "Uncle Joe, ye reckon we'uns should set the law on him?"

Hildy's father lifted his cowboy hat slightly and scratched his head with a work-hardened hand. "I don't think they could do anything, 'cause he hasn't done anything to break the law here."

"But he's a-gonna!" Ruby exploded. "He's gonna try to kid-nap Hildy and me like he done before—well, leastwise, he's fixin' to grab Hildy—and then it'll be too late, Uncle Joe!"

Mr. Corrigan thought for a minute, then shook his head again. "No, I don't think Vester's going to bother either of you girls while I'm around. What concerns me is what to do while I'm away at work."

Hildy swallowed hard, thinking the same thing. She was so concerned with the sudden reappearance of danger that she completely forgot to report on her reason for being at Lone River's only mansion.

However, her father hadn't forgotten. "I'll talk to your stepmother and decide what to do." He steered slightly toward the middle of the gravel road to avoid a long-eared jackrabbit that stepped momentarily in the path of the headlights. "Now tell us how your interview went with Farnham."

"Oh," Hildy exclaimed, "I was so worried about seeing Vester that I forgot to tell you! I don't have to wait until school starts to begin working for him part-time. Mr. Farnham wants me to help his wife take care of their two little ones on a trip from Sacramento to St. Louis. We'd leave day after tomorrow. May I go, please, Daddy?"

Before he could answer, Ruby complained, "How kin ye talk about any offer o' work when Vester's found ye?"

Hildy ignored Ruby's remark but laid a hand on her father's strong arm. "Please say yes!"

"All the way to St. Louis?" he asked doubtfully. "I suppose the Farnham's have a nice car, but still—"

"Not in a car!" Hildy broke in. "On the train! The new streamline train!"

Ruby was awed. "Y'all are a-gonna ride a steam-engine train from here clear back thar?"

Hildy nodded, eager to explain. "That's right! That's where the Farnhams will get off, because Mrs. Farnham has relatives there. Then—guess what?"

Ruby shrugged. "What?"

"Mrs. Farnham told me that she'd see to it that I get from there to the Ozarks so I can make up with Granny!"

Ruby exploded, "Ye done took leave of yore senses, Hildy? Ye go near that o'nery old woman, and she won't never let ye go!"

"She's my grandmother!" Hildy cried. "She didn't answer my letters when I asked forgiveness for coming to California last June!"

"Ye asked her to forgive ye after what she done?" Ruby cried
in disbelief. "She lied to yore stepma, and she done ye wrong
too! Yore granny's the one who should be beggin' yore forgiveness, not t'other way 'round!"

Hildy tried to be patient. "What she did is over and done,
Ruby! Oh, don't you see? This is my chance to talk with Granny
personally and patch things up, and make her understand that
my place is here with my family, not back there with her."

Ruby sighed. "I'd give a lot if'n muh daddy an' me could go.
I been a-wantin' to show him off to all them people who said I
was a woodscolt and didn't have no daddy when we lived thar."

"I wish you and Uncle Nate could go too," Hildy replied as
the headlights revealed a row of slender Lombardy poplars at
the end of the country lane. It led to the barn-house where the
Corrigan family lived because they were too poor to rent a
house.

The weak glow of a coal-oil lamp started to move inside the
barn-house. Hildy knew her stepmother had heard the approaching car, picked the light up from its usual spot on the
kitchen table, and was carrying it to the barn door. Without
electricity on the place, the lamp was needed to guide the Corrigans and Ruby after the car lights were turned off.

Hildy's father cautioned as he stopped the car, "Hildy, don't
say anything to your little sisters about Vester."

"I'll only tell Molly," Hildy promised.

Suddenly, Ruby snapped her fingers. "Hildy, I jist realized
somethin'! School starts in two weeks, and that ain't time
enough to make the trip thar an' back. So ye jist cain't go!"

The truth of that hit Hildy like a blow in the stomach. "Oh!"
she said in a weak, disappointed voice. "I completely forgot
about that!"

All her hopes were suddenly shattered, leaving her with the
terrible prospect of remaining at Lone River with Vester sneaking around somewhere, waiting—for what? Hildy suddenly felt
sick inside.

CHAPTER TWO

A SURPRISE REPORT

Hildy stepped out onto the Rickenbacker's wide running board, aware that an evening that had been so joyful at the Farnham's mansion had now gone sour. Vester's unexpected appearance had been bad enough, but Hildy had also over-looked the fact that school would start before the trip to St. Louis and back could be completed.

Hildy's stepmother Molly opened the small barn door that had been cut in the larger sliding door. She held the lamp high. As Hildy, her father, and her cousin walked toward the weak yellow glow, Hildy glimpsed her pet raccoon waddling out of the barn-house. The little masked animal passed Molly, chirring excitedly at the sight of Hildy.

"Hello, Mischief!" Hildy said, bending to pick up the little creature. The animal scrambled to her favorite perch, straddling Hildy's neck; its tiny, sensitive forepaws grasped the base of Hildy's braids, and her hind legs hung down past Hildy's throat.

"Shhh!" Molly cautioned, pressing a finger to her lips and leading the way inside and to the kitchen table. "All the kids are asleep."

The barn's northeast end had been partitioned off from the

haymow to serve as their living quarters. This single room was a combined kitchen, dining room, and bedroom. The baby, sixteen-month-old Joey, slept in the middle of a pallet of old coats and blankets between the empty icebox and the inside corner of the barn.

Another pallet was also against the same partition, but closer to the barn's front. There four towheaded sisters slept, head to toe. Their pallet occupied an area about the size of a double bed the family someday hoped to afford. Hildy slept outside on another pallet sheltered by gunnysacks.

Ruby lowered her voice. "Molly, Hildy saw Vester!"

"What?" The woman spun around, her eyes wide and her mouth open in shock.

"Put that critter down so we can talk this out, Hildy," her father said, sounding anxious.

Reluctantly, Hildy lowered her ring-tailed pet to the barn floor. "Go to your den," Hildy spoke gently but firmly, pointing toward some boxes where the coon had made herself a home. Complaining noisily, the little animal waddled across the floor.

Molly set the lamp on the crude table covered with a cracked oilcloth. Then she sat down on a bench beside her husband, while Hildy sat beside her cousin on the other bench opposite them.

In a low voice, Hildy began to explain what had happened, "After Dad dropped me off at Mr. Farnham's mansion, he and Ruby drove on to the garage where he's repairing that old Chevrolet. Mr. Farnham offered me a job. He wants me to take care of his wife and their two children on a train trip to St. Louis, where her parents live."

Molly nodded, already aware of the young wife and her two small children. Mrs. Farnham had been stricken with polio nearly two years before and was largely confined to a wheelchair. Her husband was a cattle rancher, owner of the town's only bank and a self-made, well-to-do man.

"Remember, Hildy, Molly and I haven't said you could go yet, even if school wasn't a problem," Joe Corrigan reminded his daughter.

"Git to the part about Vester," Ruby urged.

Hildy nodded and blurted out all that had transpired as she walked away from the mansion after the job interview.

When she'd finished, Molly reassured her oldest stepdaughter. "Don't worry," she said, reaching across the table to take her hand. "Vester's not going to bother you girls with both your fathers around."

Hildy stared glumly into the faintly flickering lamp flame. "I know," she said. Then after a few seconds, she added, "I want to go see Granny—but then I'd be late for school. I should be there on the first day. It's a new school in a new state!"

"I'm a-startin' the same school too, ye know," Ruby grumbled. "Only I ain't so blamed anxious to start!"

Hildy's father stood up. "Let's talk about it tomorrow night. It's time we get some sleep. I've got to be riding at sunup."

Molly rose from her place too. Hildy was thinking that her stepmother was pretty, even though her hard life had taken its toll. Molly's first husband had died in 1930. Their only child had followed him in death only two years ago.

Hildy's own mother had died in the Ozarks in May, 1933, while Hildy's father was working in Texas. For the next nine months, Hildy was substitute mother to her sisters and brother. Then her father unexpectedly took Molly as his second wife in April, this Depression year of 1934.

As Joe Corrigan left the table, Molly leaned over toward Hildy. "Let's both remember to pray about it," she suggested, smiling. She had loosened her light brown hair for the night, and it spilled over her shoulders now. A few gray strands glistened in the lamplight. Then she added, "You girls had better wash your feet and get to bed."

With a sigh, Hildy reached for her brush and comb setting on a two-by-four in the north wall, and began untying her braids. Ruby lit the lantern, and the girls walked to a cupboard made of boxes, which held a galvanized pail of water and a granite wash basin.

While Ruby held the lantern, Hildy ladled water into the basin with a long-handled dipper. Ruby took a rag towel from a nail. The family could not afford the luxury of soap.

Without speaking, the cousins stepped through the small door cut in the larger sliding door. Hildy's father blew out the lamp as soon as the girls were out, and the barn became completely dark.

Outside, Ruby sat on an upturned lug box and began washing her feet by lantern light. Hildy looked up at the sky and said a brief, silent prayer.

Ruby didn't pray, but gazed up at the stars and murmured, "Shore is purdy!"

"Beautiful!" Hildy breathed. "Looks so peaceful." Yet she had an uneasy feeling that made her glance around apprehensively. Except for the kerosene lantern, there wasn't another man-made light visible. The few rural houses in the San Joaquin Valley outside of Lone River were already dark. Ranchers went to bed early and got up before dawn.

Ruby dried her feet on the rag towel made from a barley sack. Hildy washed her feet, then threw the dirty water in a wide sweeping motion across the dusty yard.

Ruby spoke after a while, "What are ye a-gonna do 'bout the job? Go East with the Farnhams an' start school late, or what?"

Hildy considered her cousin's words while her gaze swept the peaceful countryside. Against the sky, she could see the silhouette of the stone chimney where the ranch house had burned. The long, dark shape of the tangled blackberry vines stretched away toward the open fields.

"I don't know," she answered softly. "I want to see Granny so much! I want to make up with her, but most of all I want her to understand that my place is here with my family. She's got your grandmother to keep her company back there."

Hildy's and Ruby's grandmothers were sisters, though they hadn't spoken for years. They both lived in the same little Ozark town.

Ruby snorted in the undignified way she did when she was really disgusted with something. "Them two hate each other worse'n poison!"

"I know. Oh, how I wish they'd make up!"

"More than ye want yore 'forever home' y'all are always a-talkin' about?"

"I want both," Hildy said, picking up the lantern.

"Even if'n ye got back thar, yore granny might not be nice to ye. She didn't answer yore letters or nothin'."

Hildy carried the lantern near her feet so they could see their way to the gunnysack enclosure where their pallets were. "I know."

"If'n Granny Dunnigan sent Vester to kidnap ye like she done before, an' ye went back on yore own, she might not let ye come back here never."

"Daddy'd come after me."

"He cain't afford to take time off o' work," Ruby said. "Not to mention what it'd cost to go back and fetch ye. Yore folks jist may think o' that an' not let ye go with the Farnhams."

"I've thought of that." Hildy got down on her hands and knees in front of the three-sided sack shelter against the barn. She pushed the flap aside and set the lamp inside on the dirt floor. Then she stopped. "Listen!"

She heard the distinctive sound of a Model A Ford moving slowly down the country road. It was unusual for a vehicle to be out this time of night. Hildy turned to look toward town. The car's headlights bounced up and down as the car moved slowly along.

"Probably jist some feller takin' his gal home after a date," Ruby said.

"Probably," Hildy agreed. She pushed the gunnysacks aside and crawled into the enclosure.

Ruby followed, muttering. "After the turrible things yore granny done to ye, I'd never want to see hide nor hair of her again!"

Hildy blew out the lantern so they could undress in private. "That's where you and I are different, I guess." she said simply.

"If'n she gits ye back thar alone, she prob'ly won't never let ye come back here! 'Specially if she's got Vester to he'p her keep ye!"

"Shhh!" Hildy interrupted, stiffening.

"What'd ye hear?" Ruby whispered in the darkness.

"I just realized that car going down the road has stopped. Must have turned off his lights too. I can't see them anymore." Hildy tried to control her sudden alarm. She stuck her head outside the sacks and glanced quickly up and down the road. There wasn't a sound except crickets in the nearby grass and bullfrogs in the irrigation canal across the pasture.

Ruby crawled on hands and knees to poke her head out of the shelter. "Reckon it's Vester?"

"If it is, how'd he find where we live?"

"How'd he find ye in town? In fact, how'd he find we was even in Lone River?"

"Maybe it's not Vester. Like you said, maybe it's just some young couple—stopping to spoon!"

"Maybe," Ruby agreed, "but I'll betcha it's Vester! One good thing, he won't do nothin' whilst yore daddy's around!"

"But he'll leave for work before dawn!"

"Muh daddy'll be back by then. But maybe for now, we'uns ought to sleep inside the barn."

Hildy pondered that, then shook her head. "If it is Vester sitting out there, he's just trying to scare us. He wouldn't dare come close with Daddy here."

The girls stretched out on their pallets, dressed only in their underwear fashioned from old flour sacks. The shelter was without a roof, so the girls could gaze up at the stars.

Ruby asked softly, "Ye skeered of Vester?"

"He's a dangerous man. You remember what it was like when he followed us from the Ozarks to Oklahoma, and then to Illinois—" Hildy shivered slightly. "And then grabbed us and held us prisoners in that old cattle car—"

"Reckon I 'member all that more'n I want!"

"If my grandmother didn't send him after us—and I don't think she did—then Vester wants personal revenge on us, or me."

"Ye mean 'cause we escaped after he done caught us, and that policeman done grabbed him?"

"It's more than that, I think. His pride's hurt, and he's mad."

"Yeah! No tellin' what he'll do if'n he gets the chance!"

The girls were silent. Hildy's mind flickered with countless thoughts. Finally, realizing there was nothing she could do for the present, she said a silent prayer and fell asleep.

Hildy was awakened suddenly by the sound of a car rattling down the long dirt driveway. Alarmed, Hildy sat bolt upright. It was daylight, but the sun hadn't yet risen above the trees. Ruby awoke and sat up also.

"It's muh daddy!" Ruby announced, grabbing for her shirt and overalls. "Why do ye reckon he's comin' so early?"

"Let's find out," Hildy suggested. She hastily slipped into the same dress she'd worn the day before.

The cousins stepped barefooted out of their shelter just as the topless Model T shuddered to a stop. Ruby's clean-shaven father, Nate Konning, grinned through the windshield and stepped down into the dust. He was tall and slender, with blond hair that had been parted in the middle and slicked down with hair oil.

He came toward the girls with long, quick strides. Instead of his usual scuffed cowboy boots, he wore laced leggings over shiny black shoes, and army breeches. They were olive-drab like the service breeches he had worn sixteen years ago in France during the Great War. They flared at the thighs, but fit snugly at the knees. Hildy remembered seeing them advertised in the Sears catalog for ninety-eight cents.

"Howdy," he said, in his soft Texas drawl. He doffed his sweat-stained Western hat. "I jist had me a meetin' with that thar banker feller. He likes to get up early, so we et breakfast together downtown. He done hired me as a hand."

"Oh, Daddy!" Ruby exclaimed, "That's why you wanted me to stay with Hildy last night!"

"Wasn't shore I'd get hired," her father replied, lowering his head. "Ye see, I heard he was a-lookin' for some footloose cow-puncher to ride the train back East an' play nursemaid to a prize whitefaced Hereford bull he done bought to improve his herd. 'Course I gotta ride in the cattle car with that ol' critter, but Farnham's a-payin' me enough so it's worth it."

"Yo're a-gonna go off an' leave me, then?" Ruby cried in dismay.

"How'd ye like to come along?"

"Ride the train with a big old bull?"

Hildy could see that her uncle was teasing Ruby. His grin was almost from ear to ear. "No, we'd both ride back together in a reg'lar railroad car with people. But comin' west again, I'd ride the freight train with the bull, and ye'd be on the reg'lar passenger train."

Ruby shook her head. "I don't understand."

"It's simple," Ruby's father replied. "I'm a-gonna ride the reg'lar streamliner back to St. Louis with Farnham an' his family. An' maybe ye kin come, too, honey."

Hildy's mouth dropped open in surprise. She started to explain about her job offer, but her uncle continued without a pause.

"Ye know, Mrs. Farnham is plumb stove up with a bum leg." As the girls nodded, Nate continued, "And I remembered how much muh daughter here wanted to see her hometown in the Ozarks—"

"To show ye off!" Ruby interrupted. "Make all them people back thar eat crow for all the mean things they done said about me whilst I was being raised up thar!"

"Shhh!" Hildy cautioned. "Let him finish!"

"Thankee, Hildy," Ruby's father said with mock gravity. "The truth is, Farnham told me he done offered ye a job, Hildy, help-ing take keer of his wife and two young'uns."

Hildy nodded and started to explain, but her uncle added, "This mornin' Farnham told me he decided to hire two gals— one for the kids and t'other for his wife. That means Hildy—an' one other. Maybe that's you, Ruby!"

"Me?" Ruby cried in surprised delight.

"Yep! 'Course, first ye got to go be interviewed by Mrs. Farn-ham. But if'n she hires ye, all three of us could be a-headin' for the Ozarks!"

The girls let out whoops of delight, but Hildy's caught in her throat at the sound of a Model A Ford starting up.

She glanced down the road just as a cream-colored coupe pulled off the shoulder onto the road. It made a fast U-turn and sped away.

CHAPTER
THREE

UNCLE NATE'S NEWS

Hildy stared after the Model A coupe. "That was Vester!" she exclaimed.

Ruby protested, "The driver was too far away for ye to see him plain, Hildy!"

"Just the same, I'm sure that's who it was! He must've been waiting for Daddy to leave!"

"I met Joe jist leavin' for work," Nate said. "But what're ye two gals talkin' about?"

Hildy explained about being followed in town, and then seeing the Model A stop along the road as the girls prepared for bed last night.

Ruby's father nodded thoughtfully. He had been a cowboy and sheepherder, recently called to preach the gospel. He would have to support himself by working at odd jobs. He knew of the girls' experience with Vester earlier in the summer.

Now he rubbed his smooth-shaven chin. "Seems to me if'n you gals go back to the Ozarks with me, that Vester feller won't have no call to bother y'all. So why don't ye both jist forget about him?"

"Daddy's right, Hildy!" Ruby exclaimed. "Don't jist stand

thar! Go ask yore stepmother if'n ye kin go!"

Hildy shook her head. "You're forgetting about school again. It starts in two weeks. Besides, Molly wouldn't give me permission without Daddy's agreeing to it. He probably won't let me go, on account of I'd be late starting school."

"Speakin' o' that," her uncle said, turning back to reach into the front seat, "Read this." He picked up the weekly newspaper and handed it to Hildy. "Mr. Farnham give it to me this mornin'."

Hildy looked puzzled. Then her eyes widened at the local paper's headline: *Board Postpones School Opening to September 24.*

Hildy looked up. "That's three weeks away!"

Her uncle grinned. "Yep! An' that means a whole extra week. Plenty o' time to git to the Ozarks and back here in time to start school on openin' day!"

Hildy let her eyes drop to the first paragraph. The school board had yielded to pressure from peach growers and canners and agreed to the week's delay. That would permit many teachers and older students to continue their summer jobs of picking in the orchards or working in the canneries. Without the extension, an estimated 201,000 tons of late-ripening peaches would rot, and the entire community would be affected.

Hildy looked up, her eyes brightening with hope. "Then if Daddy will let me go—"

"Now ye catch on!" Ruby interrupted. "An' with muh daddy and me a-goin' along with ye to the Ozarks, yore pa most likely'll let ye go! So go ask yore stepma if'n ye kin ride out to the ranch an' ask yore daddy now!"

"He'll probably be out on the range, riding fence or something—"

"Don't matter! We'll borry a horse an' find him!"

Hildy obtained Molly's permission to travel out to the Woods Brothers Ranch east of Lone River. About half an hour later, Nate Konning's borrowed Model T turned off the gravel county road and crossed a teeth-rattling cattle guard. The going was smoother on a dirt driveway stretched between two barbed-wire fences that led toward the low, rambling ranch house perched on a hill overlooking a creek. There was no shade by the house except for one spreading valley oak.

The bunkhouses were beyond the windmill and tankhouse. The corrals were behind them next to the barn, which sported a huge fading chewing tobacco advertisement on its side.

In all directions lay an empty expanse of low rolling hills. These marked the beginning of the foothill range leading up to the mighty Sierra Nevada Mountains. The morning breeze had died down, and though it was early September, the hot, barren land would top a hundred degrees by midafternoon.

Hildy had expected everything to be quiet because everyone would be out on the range, so she was surprised and pleased to see a man in a cowboy hat, jeans and boots swinging into the saddle of a big buckskin outside the corral.

"It's Daddy!" she cried. "His horse must have thrown a shoe or something, and he had to come back."

Joe Corrigan spurred his mount across the open area between the corral and driveway, his face showing anxiety at the unexpected appearance of his oldest daughter.

Hildy stood up in the topless car and cupped her hands to call. "Everything's okay, Daddy! I just needed to talk to you right away."

Joe Corrigan reigned in the buckskin beside the Model T and listened to Hildy's explanation and request. When she finished, her father's suntanned face clouded.

"What'd your stepmother say?" he asked.

"She says it's up to you."

"I've got to get back out on the range. I'll think on it—"

"Oh, Daddy!" Hildy moaned in disappointment.

"I'll give you my final word tonight after I talk to Molly," her father finished. He turned the buckskin's head. "Thanks for bringing her out, Nate."

On the hot, dry ride back toward Lone River, Hildy had mixed feelings of hope and doubt. *Will I get to go or not?* she asked herself over and over. *If I can't go, what'll Vester do if Ruby and Uncle Nate leave me alone while Daddy's away at work?*

Ruby's father said he'd stop at the Gilbert place where he and his daughter were staying so she could get dressed to meet

Mrs. Farnham. The handicapped woman would decide then about whether to hire Ruby to push her wheelchair while Hildy took care of the two small children.

When Ruby changed from her tomboy clothes into a new school dress and shoes, a remarkable transformation took place. "Ruby," Hildy said, "with your hair growing out, you're getting to be quite a looker!"

Ruby's father grinned as he climbed back behind the steering wheel. "Reckon I'll have to get me a bulldog to keep the boys away pretty soon."

They drove on to the barn-house where Molly suggested Hildy also get cleaned up and go with Ruby to the interview with Mrs. Farnham. Hildy would have preferred to stay home and begin thinking about what to pack in case her father decided to let her go. However, Ruby's pleading hazel eyes convinced Hildy that her cousin was afraid. It was unusual for Ruby to show any fear, but she'd never had a job interview before.

Reluctantly, Hildy put on another dress and shoes to ride along. She was glad she did, for Ruby panicked when her father stopped the Model T in front of the wrought iron gate. It was suspended from two immense brick pillars on either side of the Farnham driveway.

"I cain't go in thar!" Ruby cried, slouching down in the front seat. "I jist cain't!"

"Sure you can!" Hildy reassured her cousin. "They're nice folks! You'll like them! Besides, it's a way to get to show your father off back in the Ozarks."

Hildy jumped out to open the gate. It swung from the center on well-balanced hinges. She easily pushed the right side back against a hedge of ten-foot high oleanders with pink blossoms.

During her interview with Mrs. Farnham, Hildy had learned a little about the house. It was built in the 1920s in the Victorian style. Patterned after houses in San Francisco, the mansion had bay windows angled under the steep cabled roofs and a complicated exterior. There was a tower at the left front of the house that rose past the third story, even higher than several chimneys.

While Uncle Nate drove the car through the gate, Hildy stud-

ied the house, which was painted a somber gray. It stood ma-
jestically in the center of three acres of shade trees that gave the
grounds the appearance of a park.

When the motor was again idling, Hildy closed the gate and
climbed back into the Model T. It moved slowly up the paved
driveway lined with old Dutch elm and sycamore trees. They
provided welcome shade from the blistering sun.

Ruby's nervousness expressed itself in a giggle. "Hildy,
what's a couple of gals like us from the Ozarks doin' in a place
like this?"

Hildy smiled at her cousin. "Someday I'm going to have a
house like this. It's very nice inside, with lots of handmade furniture and everything."

Ruby seemed to be losing her fear. "Ye reckon maybe someday this'll be yore place? Yore 'forever home'?"

Hildy shook her head, and her brown braids swished back
and forth. "It's beautiful, but too big. I just want something
permanent, so we won't ever have to move again."

She was silent a moment, remembering the countless times
her father had moved the family from one state to another, looking for work. The Corrigans had lived in the barn-house a couple
of months. Hildy never spoke of it, but she had a secret dread
of her father arriving home from work some evening and an-
nouncing they were moving again. Hildy shook her head
sharply, trying to drive the scary thought away.

The Model T eased under a porch open at both ends. Hildy
explained, "Mrs. Farnham said this was the carriage entrance.
When people still had horses and buggies, they could drive right
under here and walk into the house without getting wet when
it rained."

Hildy started to get out of the car, but Ruby hesitated. She
glanced around anxiously at the immense house and acres of
green, perfectly kept lawns and flower beds. Roses grew everywhere. "Why don't we come back another time?" she suggested.

Hildy smiled and pulled on her cousin's arm. "There's no
time! And don't be scared!"

"I'm not skeered!"

"Then come on!" Hildy urged. She led the way up the few wooden stairs to a large screened-in porch that ran the entire length of the house.

"Mr. Farnham had this part added so the kids could have a place to play in the winter," Hildy explained. "I understand it rains hard around here, and sometimes terrible fogs come in."

Ruby's father stepped up and twisted a handle in the middle of a frosted-glass windowed door.

Hildy heard the bell ringing somewhere deep inside the mansion.

"What'll I say?" Ruby groaned, glancing around anxiously. "I ain't never talked to no grand lady!"

"Don't worry! Both Mr. and Mrs. Farnham told me they were born poor, just like us! They said that in America, a person who really wants it, can have anything—like this house."

"Even in the Depression?" Ruby's father asked.

Hildy nodded. "Mrs. Farnham told me that she and her husband bought this place just before the Crash of 1929. Most banks across the country went broke and had to close, but Mr. Farnham's little bank made it."

Ruby's father gave the bell handle another twist. "Probably on account of he had lots of land and cattle holdings."

Hildy thought that made sense. She turned to look across the lawns toward the river. A faint fragrance of willows and cottonwoods tickled her nose.

"This is shore about the purdiest spot in this whole blessed country," Ruby's father mused.

Hildy turned back as she heard the front door open. In the shadows of the house's interior, Hildy recognized Matthew Farnham through the screen door. He was a small, dapper man, nattily dressed in a light tan summer suit and white shoes. Looking over the top of rectangular, silver-framed glasses, he greeted Hildy and Nate.

They returned the greeting, and Nate introduced his daughter. The banker opened the screen door and invited the visitors in.

Two children dashed from the darkened interior. Hildy bent

down and held out her arms. The older blond-haired boy rushed into them with a glad cry, but his younger sister shyly hid behind her father's legs.

Hildy introduced the children, "Uncle Nate, Ruby—this is Dickie. He's six. And this is Constance—Connie. She's not quite four. Dickie, Connie, this is my Uncle Nate and my cousin Ruby."

Ruby had been staring openmouthed at the ornate ceiling frescoes and dark, heavy furniture illuminated by one immense gaslight fixture of embossed brass and delicate, flowered glass shades.

Ruby knelt down to smile at the children, who regarded her somberly. "Hi," Ruby said.

Dickie was very fair, with masses of yellow curls and large blue eyes. His sister's eyes were not so large, but were every bit as blue. Her hair was straight and very blonde—almost white.

When Hildy had come for her interview, the children's mother had said with a sigh that she wished the curly blond hair and large eyes belonged to the girl.

"My wife is coming," Mr. Farnham announced.

Hildy stood up, her hands resting on the children's shoulders as Mrs. Farnham wheeled up in her chair. The rich Persian rug that ran the length of the hallway afforded a soft cushion so that the wheels made almost no sound.

"Hildy, how nice to see you again!" Mrs. Farnham said with a smile. The sight of her made Hildy think of a fragile china doll she'd seen behind the beveled-glass doors of a hutch in the dining room of the mansion.

Mrs. Farnham was blonde with almost transparent white skin. Tiny blue veins could be seen near the surface. The dark circles under her eyes and lines on her young face revealed the toll polio had taken. Hildy tried not to stare at Mrs. Farnham's left leg, thin as a matchstick beneath her flowered summer skirt.

After a moment, the banker suggested he show Nate around the place while Mrs. Farnham and Ruby discussed their business. Hildy volunteered to take Dickie and Connie to play on the swings. As Hildy walked outside with the children, she whispered, "You'll do just fine, Ruby!"

"I shore hope so!" Ruby replied softly.

As Hildy entered the yard, she walked past a gnarled old fig tree to the deep shade of a silver maple. There a two-rope swing with a notched board seat wide enough for two awaited them. She had never known anything but a tire swing suspended from a single rope, so she enjoyed this one where she could sit with one child at a time, or swing the two of them together.

Hildy had a natural way with children, so it was easy for her to keep them contented. They laughed and called, "My turn!" Hildy kept an eye on the house, wondering how Ruby was doing.

"She's just got to get that job!" Hildy whispered fiercely to herself. "She wants so very much to show people back in the Ozarks that she really does have a father!"

Her mind jumped again, her emotions stirring with the intensity of her feelings. *And I want to go with her! Oh, Daddy's just got to let me! But if—I mean, when—I get back there, there's so much to do!*

Hildy absently gave Connie another push in the swing, but her mind was on the problem at hand. *What if Granny won't forgive me? What if she won't see that I belong here? What if she uses Vester to keep me there against my will? And if I stay here, Vester will cause trouble! When Daddy's at work, and Uncle Nate's back East, what will Vester do to me?*

Hildy shivered at the idea of that crude, tobacco-chewing moonshiner kidnapping her again. Her insides churned until she heard the screen door squeak open. Hildy glanced up as Ruby stepped into view.

"Dickie, Connie!" Hildy exclaimed, grabbing each child by the hand. "Let's go see if Ruby got the job! If she did—"

Hildy didn't finish the sentence. So much depended on what news her cousin had. Hildy ran as fast as the children allowed across the yard to where Ruby stood in the shadow of the carriage entrance.

CHAPTER
FOUR
——

A QUIET THREAT

Hildy was almost to the carriage entrance before Ruby stepped out of the shadows. Her golden hair glistened in the sun. She was smiling.

"I got me the job!" Ruby shouted, reaching out toward Hildy. "Mrs. Farnham's reg'lar he'p cain't make the trip, so she done hired me to go along on the train and push her wheelchair!"

Hildy let go of the children's hands to grip Ruby's. "Oh, I'm so glad!"

Ruby spoke to the children. "Yore ma says for ye both to come in now."

They obeyed instantly, and when they'd disappeared inside the house, Ruby glanced around. "Where's muh daddy?"

"He and Mr. Farnham are out by the barn." Hildy started walking in that direction.

Ruby swung in beside her. "Me 'n' him got to git home an' pack, 'cause we leave day after tomorrow!"

Hildy stopped short in surprise. "Day after—?"

"Uh-huh!" Ruby kept walking. "Oh, jist wait'll them mean ol' folks back in Possum Holler see me walk in with muh daddy! I'll learn them to say such turrible things about me! 'Specially Bertha Killian."

Hildy frowned, remembering the dreaded name. "Big Bertha! I haven't thought of her in months."

"I shore have! She was always pickin' on me and sayin' nasty things."

"Me, too," Hildy admitted. "She and her friend, Iris Hastings!"

"I heard tell Bertha got her name from that gun the so'jer boys used in France. Her friend Iris ain't so big, but she's got a mean streak in her."

Hildy shook her head. "I think Iris is just mad at the world because she's an orphan and was reared by her grandfather."

"Oh yeah! Brother Rufus Hurley, the preacher man. Maybe Iris don't like being a preacher's kid any more'n I do."

"I thought you felt better about that since your dad got such a big response at his first sermon on Thunder Mountain."

"Warn't he somethin'?" Ruby asked with pride. "He done turned the whole church upside down!"

As the girls approached the gate leading from the park-like estate to the barn, Ruby returned to the subject of Bertha and Iris. "Wonder how many fights me 'n' ol' Bertha had?"

"I couldn't even begin to guess!"

"Anyhow," Ruby added, "This time it'll be different with Bertha and Iris on account o' muh daddy'll be there! Not that I couldn't whup 'em both if need be."

"You're getting too old to roll around in the dirt and pull hair and such things," Hildy said.

Ruby laughed. "Maybe I won't have to! I jist thought of somethin!" She glanced down at her print dress, and lightly touched her blonde hair. It was still short like a boy's, but was starting to grow out.

"What's that?" Hildy asked.

Ruby's face split into a grin, but there was mischief in her eyes. "Ye remember Bertha was always sort of sweet on Elston Edwards, secret-like, I mean?"

Hildy nodded. Elston was the bully of Possum Hollow's one-room school where Hildy and Ruby attended before moving to California.

"Elston was always takin' Bertha's side." Ruby complained. "Like the time we was playin' 'Annie Over' an' she and me ran into each other racin' around the corner of the schoolhouse."

Hildy again nodded. "You hit so hard, you were both knocked down. Then you got into a fight like a couple of boys."

"I'da whupped her good if'n Elston hadn't come along and he'ped Bertha!" Ruby interrupted. "Only now I got me a idee of how to get even with both of them!"

"How?"

"They ain't never seen me in no dress. So supposin' I jist sorta made calves' eyes at Elston, and Bertha saw me?"

Hildy shook her head. "Bertha'd be all over you again!"

"Maybe not! Suppose ol' Elston'd sorta cottoned to the idee of me a-smilin' nice at him? An' if'n he did, that'd burn Bertha up! An' would I love that!"

"I don't think that's such a good idea."

"I kin hardly wait to see everybody's faces when they meet muh daddy! Hildy, I shore hope you can be thar with me! Maybe yore daddy'll let ye go to he'p take keer of them two little kids!"

Hildy sighed wistfully. "I hope so!"

The girls found Ruby's father and Matthew Farnham standing in the shade of the barn, looking out across the river while they talked. Ruby announced happily that the Farnhams had hired her.

Hildy was glad for her cousin and eager to go with her, but she also still felt the same nagging sense of concern. Suppose her father wouldn't let her go? And what would Vester do if she stayed in Lone River?

On the drive back to the barn-house in the open Model T, the girls removed their shoes to protect them.

"Ye know what?" Ruby mused. "Mrs. Farnham says she come from a background like mine, and she learned to talk like a lady, so she wants I should, too. Hildy, ye reckon ye could he'p me talk better?"

Hildy nodded, remembering how she had determined to speak properly and with only the faintest hint of an accent. "I'd be happy to help," she said.

Nate Konning shifted his hands on the steering wheel and turned to look at the girls riding beside him. "Hildy's already a-teachin' me—I mean—already teaching me—to talk better. It ain't—it's not proper for a preacher to speak in such a way that don't honor God."

"Doesn't," Hildy corrected gently. "You asked me to tell you when you made a mistake, Uncle Nate."

"I'm obliged to ye—you, Hildy," he replied solemnly.

Ruby smiled broadly. "Maybe by the time we reach the Ozarks, Hildy'll have us talkin' so good that people back home'll think we talk plumb funny!"

Hildy smiled too. "I don't think there's much chance of that! Anyway, we don't know yet if my father'll let me go along."

"He'll let ye—you," her uncle assured her solemnly. "I been a-prayin'—uh, I've been praying for you to go, Hildy. I know how much it means for ye to make up with your grandmother."

"I appreciate your prayers," Hildy said. "Daddy'll be home in just a few hours, and then I'll find out."

They were driving through Lone River's downtown business section when Nate Konning unexpectedly pulled the Model T over to the high curb in front of the town's only combination drugstore and soda fountain.

"Seein' that sign in the window there—'five pack razor blades, six cents,' reminds me I need some," he explained. "You gals want to come with me or sit here?"

Ruby exclaimed, "Hildy, let's go shoppin'! Mrs. Farnham give me five dollars to pick up whatever I need." Ruby produced the bill for inspection. "Meetcha back here directly, Daddy!"

The barefooted girls ran down a side street to a women's shop. A sign in the window read: "Silk dresses, two for $4.77."

The girls entered the store. Ruby showed her five-dollar bill to the store owner, chose a couple of dresses, and entered a small changing booth to try them on.

From behind the curtain, Ruby mused, "Wonder if'n ol' Elston'll like me in this dress."

Hildy shook her head in wonderment at her cousin's changing attitude. As long as Hildy could remember, Ruby had been a tomboy. Now she was not only wearing a dress, but wondering if a boy would like it.

Hildy wandered around the store, trying to remember the last time she'd had a store-bought dress. Her mother had always made the girls' clothes before she died, and now Hildy's step-mother was helping Hildy sew her own.

Near the front window, Hildy suddenly stopped stock still, her eyes focused on a man walking past the window.

That looked like Vester! she told herself, feeling her heart speed up. For a moment, Hildy hesitated, then impulsively dashed out the door.

The man in overalls was just turning the corner, but Hildy caught a quick glimpse of a heavyset person with a black slouch hat.

"I've got to be sure!" Hildy told herself, breaking into a run. Her bare feet were almost silent on the concrete sidewalk. She dashed around the corner and stopped in sudden fear. "Vester!"

His pockmarked forehead was visible under his hat. His red-dish beard split in the familiar, evil grin Hildy remembered so well. His yellow teeth showed as he shifted a wad of chewing tobacco from his left check to the right.

"I figured ye'd come a-bustin' out o' that thar store if'n I give ye a little look at me," he said. He fingered the rabbit's foot dangling from the breast pocket of his patched blue overalls.

Hildy took a couple of steps backward to stay out of reach. Tensed to run, she demanded, "What do you want?"

The mountaineer studied Hildy with menacing dark eyes under heavy reddish-brown eyebrows. "I come to give ye a choice," he replied, his eyes glittering with the same steady intensity Hildy had seen in a snake's eyes. "Either come back peaceable with me to yore ol' granny, or I'll take ye back the hard way."

Hildy tried to ignore the threat. "Did my grandmother send you after me?" She asked.

Vester shifted uneasily and shook his head. "I come on muh own 'cause I still got a score to settle with Ruby and ye for what ye done to me before."

Hildy squinted sternly at him. "I don't think you came on your own! I think Granny threatened you with one of her hexes, and you're scared of that!"

"I ain't skeered o' that ol' granny woman!"

"I think you are, but that's silly because she can't put a curse on you or anybody else! It's all in your imagination!"

"Ain't muh 'magination," Vester replied. "She's got a power like nobody else in them hills!"

Hildy sensed this big man was afraid of a tiny old mountain woman's imagined power to put spells on people. Hildy said, "I think Granny told you she'd put a hex on you because Ruby and I got away from you this summer. She might've even said you'd be hexed until you died if you didn't bring me back. Isn't that right?"

Vester's fingers moved more rapidly over the rabbit's foot as though seeking protection from it. "Think yo're purdy smart, don't ye, Hildy?"

"Granny was just trying to scare you!" Hildy protested, ignoring her desire to run in hopes she could talk this superstitious man out of his foolish ideas. "You're not cursed!"

With obvious reluctance, Vester admitted that Hildy had guessed right. "Yeah, I'm hexed. She tol' me plain. Only way I can get shut of it is to bring ye back. So I'm a-gonna do it. Now, ye comin' peaceable?"

Hildy glanced around nervously, hoping some other people were nearby. "My father'll never let you take me!" she warned. "If you try, he and Uncle Nate'll make you real sorry! They'd have the law on you too!"

The mountaineer shrugged. "That don't skeer me."

Hildy realized that was true. The unreasoning fear and belief in an old woman's words carried more power with Vester than fear of the men or the law.

Hildy also realized something else. *I was so scared when he kidnapped Ruby and me this summer, but he's the one that's afraid now! He's so afraid of that hex that he's liable to do something desperate.*

Hildy also knew it was useless to try reasoning with Vester. She turned to run. "You leave me alone!" she cried.

"Cain't do that, Hildy, and ye know it!" Vester's voice was deadly quiet and threatening. "I also heard tell about Ruby findin' her pa, but that ain't gonna stop me from taking ye both back."

"Both?" Hildy forced herself to stand still when every fiber of her being wanted to run away.

"Uh-huh."

"Why're you bothering Ruby?" Hildy demanded angrily.

The man shrugged again. "That's muh business. Now, I done give ye a chance. Y'all a-comin' along with me now, nice and peaceable, or—?"

Hildy didn't wait for him to finish. She suddenly broke into a hard, fast run. As she rounded the corner, she saw Ruby standing in the doorway of the store, looking up and down the street. Hildy didn't even slow up but grabbed her cousin's hand as she ran by.

"Vester's after us! Come on! Let's get back to your father, fast!"

Ruby was almost jerked off balance, but she quickly regained it and ran barefooted beside Hildy.

Ruby glanced back. "I don't see him!"

Hildy twisted her head to look over her shoulder. Vester was nowhere in sight. With a sigh, Hildy slowed and let go of Ruby's wrist. "He was there, I tell you! I talked to him right around the corner! He says he's come to take both of us back to the Ozarks because Granny put a curse on him!"

"Didja tell him ye might be a-goin' back with me and muh daddy?"

"Never thought of it! But I did think of something else. Maybe it's because I've grown up a little. But I could see that he's as afraid of Granny as we've been of him. People do mean and cruel things sometimes because they've got a big problem. And frightened people can be dangerous!"

"Ye mean, Vester kin be dangerous—to *both* of us?"

"I'm afraid so."

"When he grabbed us in Illinois and hid us in that old railroad car, he skeered me plenty! I still git goose bumps thinkin' o' the way he looked at me. So what do ye reckon he's gonna do if'n he catches us again?"

"We can't let him catch us! If I get to see Granny, maybe I can get her to tell Vester there's no hex on him! Then he'd leave us alone."

The girls ran back to the Model T just as Nate came out of the drugstore. Hildy told him about talking to Vester, but when Nate drove around the corner to look for him, there was no sign of the mountaineer.

"May as well take me home, I guess," she said. "I want to be there when Daddy gets off work."

"When ye tell him about Vester," Ruby said, "do ye reckon Uncle Joe'll let ye go with Daddy an' me? Be safer."

"I don't know. But without you and Uncle Nate around, I'd be scared to stay here."

The Model T headed into the country, taking Hildy to where she would soon know her father's decision.

CHAPTER
FIVE
—

DISAPPOINTMENT AND HOPE

It was nearing dusk when Hildy heard her father's Ricken-backer coming up the long, dusty driveway.

All five Corrigan daughters ran out to greet their father. Hildy dashed ahead, anxious to know his decision about allowing her to go East. She was less anxious to tell about her conversation with Vester, but she knew that also had to be done.

But one glance at her father's face told her something was wrong. He confirmed this by sticking his head out the open window as his daughters approached him. He yelled, "Stay back!"

"Oh-oh!" Hildy whispered in alarm as her four little sisters fell silent. "He's in a bad mood!"

He parked the long black sedan by an oil drum resting on a raised platform. He jumped out of the driver's seat and slammed the door hard.

Hildy stood uncertainly looking at her father as he glumly approached the raised fuel tank.

Elizabeth, two years younger than Hildy, whispered to her,

"What do you suppose happened?"

"I don't know."

Countless fathers in the depths of the Depression frequently came home angry and depressed. That was understandable, for there had been five years of hard times, with no end in sight. Last year, Hildy knew more than sixteen million men were unemployed, so her father was fortunate to even be working. What few jobs there were paid very low wages.

Joe Corrigan earned $15 dollars a week, or $780 a year, riding sunup to sundown six days a week on a cattle ranch. There were no vacations, and if he was fired, a dozen men stood ready to take his job. It was very difficult to be happy and carefree, especially for a family man.

On several occasions, driving through Lone River on a Saturday night, Hildy had heard women screaming and kids shrieking. Molly had explained to Hildy that men were beating up on their wives and kids out of frustration. That, along with the usual Saturday night bath, was becoming common in the poorer sections of town.

Hildy's father sometimes drank, and when he did, he yelled and swore something fierce, but he hadn't yet done anything so awful as beat his wife and children. In past years, when he'd come home sullen and silent, it often meant he had lost his job and the family would be moving on again. If that was true now, Hildy knew there'd be no trip to the Ozarks.

Hildy prayed earnestly that her father's job was not being threatened. Then she approached him slowly, her four towheaded sisters remaining silent until they knew the cause of their father's behavior.

Without a word, he removed the short hose end from the oil drum and walked toward the rear of the car with the hose.

He had recently traded his "shade tree" mechanical labor for the car. It had been manufactured by Eddie Rickenbacker, the American aviation ace in the Great War that had ended sixteen years before. The long, eight-cylinder vehicle was a gas-guzzler, averaging only five miles per gallon. But Joe Corrigan had found a way to beat that problem.

On Sundays, his only day off from work, he had laboriously synchronized the Rickenbacker's dual ignition system so that it would both start and run on stove oil, which cost only three cents a gallon, while gasoline cost twelve cents. Converting the Rickenbacker to run on stove oil had helped to stretch Joe's daily $2.50 income.

Hildy's father had explained to her that it was illegal for a service station attendant to put stove oil in a car, so Joe had arranged for the oil truck driver to deliver a fifty-five gallon drum to the barn-house yard.

Through the gathering dusk, Hildy gingerly stepped closer to her father's side as he inserted the oil hose into the car's thirty-gallon tank by the rear spare tire. Then she noticed that both sleeves of her father's blue work shirt were ripped, and the backs of his work-callused hands were caked with dried blood.

She gasped. "Daddy! What happened?"

Her four younger sisters, surprised by Hildy's question, strained to see what she saw without disturbing their father.

He answered in a weary voice, "Oh, I was just helping another rider repair some barbed wire where the cattle had gotten out, and he let the wire get away from him. It coiled back and caught me."

Somehow, Hildy didn't think that was reason enough for her father's gloomy demeanor. She wondered if there was something else he wasn't telling.

While she pondered it all, Martha spoke up, "You should have worn gloves, Daddy!"

"Can't afford them!" he snapped, "They cost 39 cents a pair! Anyway, it wouldn't have helped," he muttered. "When wire gets away, it coils like a spring and moves faster than a striking rattlesnake. See how it ripped my shirtsleeves? Just lucky it didn't get my face!"

Martha started to sob over her father's sharp tone, but he was too preoccupied to notice.

Hildy herded her sisters away, saying gently, "Let's get some water in a pan so Daddy can wash up."

It wasn't in their father's nature to apologize easily. He glowered at the hose in sullen silence while continuing to fill the car's tank.

Hildy had realized it was no time to discuss her pressing need for his decision about going to the Ozarks, but five-year-old Sarah blurted it out as they headed for the barn, "Daddy," she called, "Uncle Nate and Ruby got a job and they're going on the train. Can Hildy go with them?"

Joe Corrigan's head snapped up sharply, almost flipping his cowboy hat from his head. The hard set of his jaw was visible in the dusk. "No! Nobody's going *no* place!"

"But, Daddy!" Hildy wailed without thinking, "I've got to go!"

"Don't tell me what you've got to do, young lady!" He hung the hose back on the oil drum and screwed the cap back on the gas tank.

Hildy turned and walked back to her father, trailed by the solemn sisters. "Please don't be angry," Hildy pleaded. "At least listen to me!"

"I'm in no mood to listen to anything! Supper ready?"

Behind her, Hildy heard eleven-year-old Elizabeth whisper to Sarah. "See what you did? Now Daddy won't let Hildy go, and it's your fault!"

Sarah let out a squeal. "I didn't mean to!"

Hildy bent down to comfort her little sister. "It's all right, Sarah." Hildy said sadly. "It's nobody's fault. Daddy's hurting, and he didn't mean anything by it. Now go with the others. Soon's Daddy's washed up, we'll have supper."

Hildy's disappointment was so intense it seemed to settle like a heavy stone pressing on her insides. Still, she was more determined than ever, and her mind whirled furiously with possible ways to achieve her goal. But no answers came until the meal of pinto beans, boiled potatoes, and fresh biscuits was served.

There was a strained silence at the plank table. The cracked oilcloth covering seemed more bleak than ever, and the weak light from the kerosene lamp in the middle of the table seemed to reflect everyone's mood. The six children faced one another

around the table on the crude homemade benches. Joe Corrigan
was seated at the end of the table nearest the barn door, on an
upturned nail keg. Molly sat at the other end on a dilapidated
ladder-back chair near the kitchen range.

"Daddy," Hildy began bravely, laying her fork on the plate
and looking straight at him, "I talked to Vester today."

The sullen look on Joe Corrigan's face changed to one of
instant concern. "You what?"

Hildy explained briefly, carefully following the plan she'd
worked out to get her father to change his mind. Then she concluded, "So when Vester asked, 'Are you coming along with
me?' I turned and ran."

Joe Corrigan's fork dropped to his plate with a clatter. He
slammed his strong right hand down so hard on the end of the
table that the lamp jumped. Molly grabbed the glass base to
steady it, while Joe shook his hand to relieve the smarting from
the cuts that he'd forgotten about in his anger.

"I've got to catch up to that weasel and whup his o'nery
hide!" he growled. Joe tended to lapse into Ozark speech when
he was angry. "I'll teach him to go 'round threatenin' muh family!"

Hildy judged that the time had come to risk her plan. "If you
let me go with the others on the train, Vester'd have no reason
to bother me, because I'd voluntarily be going to see Granny
Dunnigan."

Her father shook his head. "If you were back there, she might
team up with that no-account Vester to keep you there," he
reasoned. "I could come get you, of course—and I would—but
I'd lose my job, and then there'd be the expense of traveling—
and dealing with that wretch of a man *and* your grand—"

Hildy knew she shouldn't interrupt her father, but she was
too anxious to resolve her dilemma. "I'd be safe with Ruby and
Uncle Nate. Nobody could stop me from coming back here with
three of us there! Oh, don't you see, Daddy? Letting me go would
be the easiest way to solve this whole problem!"

He opened his mouth as if to reply, then slowly closed it.
"I'll talk to Molly and let you know in the morning."

At least he didn't turn me down flat! Hildy told herself hopefully.

It was a long night for Hildy. Because Ruby wasn't with her, Hildy decided not to risk sleeping outside. But it was hot in the barn-house, and her mind was so busy she couldn't sleep. She tried to pet her raccoon, but the little animal was hot too, and moved off seeking a cooler spot. Hildy prayed silently, trying to imagine her prayers already answered and herself walking up to her grandmother's door.

Wonder how she'll react? Hildy thought, staring into the darkness above her. *Will she understand and be nice to me for once, or run me off like a stray cat?*

Granny Dunnigan was unpredictable, but Hildy was counting on her grandmother having enough love to at least allow Hildy time to apologize for running off in June.

"No matter what she does," Hildy told herself, as an owl hooted softly from the hay mow, "I won't have a guilty conscience anymore if I can just talk to her. I need to make her understand why I have to be with my family."

Hildy usually didn't hear her father's footsteps as he crept out of the cramped sleeping quarters before dawn, but this morning she sat up at the first sound of his boots on the barn floor.

"Daddy?" she whispered, so as not to wake her sleeping siblings. "What'd you and Molly decide?"

"Walk out to the car with me," he whispered back, putting on his cowboy hat.

Hildy quickly slipped her dress over her head and walked barefooted outside. There was always a light breeze in the San Joaquin Valley on a summer morning. Even now, as September was upon them, the pleasant breeze caressed Hildy's face. A mourning dove called from a nearby almond orchard. It was a sad, lonely sound, but pleasant too. Hildy's heart beat faster as she looked up at her father, awaiting his response.

"It was a hard decision for your stepmother and me," he began slowly, "but we've decided you'll be safer with Nate and Ruby than you'd be around here while I'm away at work."

"Oh, thank you, thank you!" Hildy blurted, jumping to her tiptoes and kissing her father quickly on his stubbly cheek.

"But there's one thing more, Hildy," he added uneasily.

"Yes?" she prompted, remembering her thoughts last night about his not telling the real reason he was so cranky.

"The boss is going to have to lay off some riders."

Her heart sank. "Not you?"

"I don't know yet. He just told us yesterday. Said times are just too hard for him to pay all of us. He wanted to know if anyone had another job offer, but of course no one had."

"Oh, Daddy! If he lets you go, will we have to move again?"

"We have to move anyway, Hildy." He took off his hat and bowed his head. "I can't afford this place anymore." His voice sounded choked as he glanced toward the barn-house. "By the time you get back from the Ozarks, we'll likely be packed."

Hildy's heart sank. "But where'll we go?" she whispered, almost afraid to speak. "Not back to Texas, or the Ozarks? Oh, Daddy, California's the place where I know we'll find our 'forever home' someday!"

"Maybe Oregon," he said wistfully, reaching out and pulling his daughter close to him, almost crushing her in a powerful embrace. "But don't you fret! Just go make up with your grandmother and come back safe and sound. You hear?"

Hildy nodded, her eyes filling with tears.

In no time her father was in the car and down the driveway. Hildy stared after him, her heart filled with joy and pain together. Then she turned and ran misty-eyed toward the barn-house.

Elizabeth stood in the doorway in her flour-sack nightgown. "What'd he say, Hildy? Can you go to the Ozarks?"

"Yes! Shhh! You'll wake our sisters!"

"You're coming back, aren't you? You won't let Granny keep you there? Or that mean old Vester?"

"Nothing's going to keep me from coming back!" Hildy said firmly. But suddenly a strange feeling came over her that maybe she was fooling herself—that if she left, she'd never get to come back to her family.

CHAPTER
SIX
———

BACK TO THE OZARKS

After whirlwind preparations, Hildy, Ruby, and her father were ready for the trip. The girls each had a small cardboard suitcase. Ruby's father had a wicker one. The girls both wore shoes and dresses when Mr. Farnham stopped by the barnhouse to pick up his passengers in his Pierce Arrow.

The dapper cattleman-banker drove them with his wife and two children to the county seat, fifteen miles from Lone River. There the girls saw their shabby cardboard suitcases loaded aboard the train with the Farnhams' fine luggage. But Hildy and Ruby didn't care, for this was their first time ever to be on a train.

They ate in the dining car that night, helped get Mrs. Farnham and the two children settled in a Pullman car, then went exploring, while Nate and the banker talked business.

The cousins moved through the string of cars with their many empty seats. Even though Hildy didn't know for certain what the Farnhams paid for the seven tickets to St. Louis, she had seen ads in the daily newspaper for tickets from Sacramento to New York by train. The prices were $107.20, tourist, and $124.50, first class. Times were too hard for many people to travel by train, and for this reason the coaches were only partly filled.

The girls quickly adjusted to the swaying coaches, learning to walk without holding on to the backs of seats as they passed. Hildy liked the pleasant, steady rhythm of the big steel wheels clickety-clacking on the iron rails. The steam locomotive's whistle sounded lonesome and far away, as the train approached an unguarded crossing.

Through the windows, against the blackness of the night, Hildy glimpsed the campfires and meager shelters of a hobo jungle. Mr. Farnham had explained to them earlier that this was where desperate, disheartened men who had "ridden the rails" seeking jobs huddled together at night along the tracks.

Hildy wore one of the two practical but nice dresses she had purchased for $1.95 each with the $5.00 Mrs. Farnham had given her. She felt confident having $1.10 still in her pocket. She'd left two dresses at home that Molly had made for her to wear to school and to church.

Ruby had put on one of the silk dresses she'd bought with her five dollars, and both girls wore their new school shoes, which were rather tight and uncomfortable on feet that had been bare since spring.

As they moved through the dining car where they had eaten supper with the Farnhams, Ruby said, "Didja ever see such nice things? I mean, all them purdy silver knives an' forks and suchlike! An' them colored men with their white jackets takin' our orders an' servin' dishes like we was richer'n a king! An' nobody calls us poor white trash, hillbillies, Okies or Arkies."

Hildy nodded, remembering how hurt she'd felt when people called her names like that. But she knew it was nothing compared to the way some people were treated, especially in certain areas of the country.

Hildy spoke her thoughts to her friend, "I remember Daddy telling me about an awful sign he saw once in the South. It said, 'Nigger, don't let the sun set on you in this town!' "

Ruby mused, "When ye learn me to speak good, without no accent, reckon nobody'll know you 'n' me's jist plain ol' country gals?"

Hildy gently corrected her cousin's English, as Ruby had asked her to.

"It'll be quite a spell afore—I mean, before I speak like a lady," Ruby said.

Hildy smiled, remembering her own determination to lose her accent and speak properly. "I believe you can do anything you really want to," she spoke confidently, "providing it's in line with God's will, of course."

"Now, don't start talkin' religion to me! Ye know how I feel about that!"

"Okay, but I think it's mighty important."

The girls were struggling to open the heavy doors between the end of one car and the next when Hildy glanced over her shoulder and suddenly froze.

Ruby, facing the door, cried, "Whatcha tryin' to do? Turn me into mashed 'taters?"

Hildy ignored her cousin's remark and whispered, "Did you see him?"

Ruby let the door slide shut. "See who?"

"Vester!"

Ruby's voice registered her alarm. *"Where?"*

"Back there! He was standing in the other car, watching us through the doors. When he saw me turn around and look at him, he ducked back out of sight."

"Ye shore?"

"Yes! Well—I think I'm sure."

"How'd he get on this train without us knowing it?"

"How should I know? Let's find out!"

Hildy hurried through the car, back the way they'd come, followed by her protesting cousin. At the far end of the car, Hildy peered through the windows before opening the door. With Ruby's help, she slid it open, stepped onto the next car and forced that door open, her heart beating harder with every step.

Both girls stopped and looked around. Hildy's blue eyes skimmed the seats, but nobody looked anything like the heavy-set mountaineer.

"He's gone!" she said, her mouth suddenly dry from fear.

The far end of the car opened and a "butcher boy" wearing a cap and apron entered, calling, "Newspapers! Candy bars! Get yours here!"

Hildy hurried to speak to him. "Did you see a heavyset man in overalls and a black hat in that car?"

"You crazy, kid?" the boy asked scornfully. He wasn't much older than Hildy. "Everybody on here's wearin' a suit, 'though I admit some of 'ems mighty worn and thin."

Hildy thanked the boy, who pressed on down the car, hawking his wares. Hildy looked at Ruby, voicing her doubt, "Maybe it wasn't Vester. Maybe I'm just so concerned about his threats and how desperate he is that I imagined I saw him."

"Reckon yo're right. Ain't no place on this train that a body could hide for a couple thousand miles."

In spite of reassuring themselves, the cousins walked back with watchful eyes. They passed porters lowering the seats to make upper and lower bunks for sleeping. There were two small lights in the back corners and one overhead. There were even window shades that pulled down, just like in a house.

"I feel a little foolish," Hildy told Ruby as they neared the Farnham's Pullman. "I probably didn't see Vester, so let's not say anything to anybody."

"Not even muh daddy?"

"Not even him."

Still, Hildy decided to keep a sharp eye out on the rest of the trip. And she had plenty of opportunity to do that as the train rolled east, because the two young children were restless and liked to roam from car to car. But there was no more sign of Vester.

Ruby had some trouble with Mrs. Farnham's wheelchair, because the train wasn't made for it. But the woman was patient and kind, and both her husband and Ruby's father helped.

On their last evening, knowing they would reach St. Louis early the next morning, Hildy quit thinking about Vester. Instead, she thought how she would make up with her strong-willed grandmother. Hildy leaned back in an empty seat and closed her eyes.

Awed by her first train trip, Ruby was babbling. She marveled about the way Mr. Farnham left his shoes outside his compartment each night and found them neatly polished the next morning. She mentioned talking to a couple who'd traveled across country before. This time, they were going to try the new way back to California.

Ruby said with wonder in her tone, "Ye know what he said, Hildy? He said he and his missus go on to New York by train, then, comin' back, they'll fly in an airplane by day and change to the train at night. He says, soon people will fly all the way from New York to Californy. Can ye imagine sich a thing?"

"We live in a wonderful age," Hildy said without real interest. Her eyes were still closed.

Ruby's tone changed to one of concern, "Ye skeered about what yore o'nery old Granny's a-gonna do when ye show up on her doorstep?"

"A little," Hildy admitted. "How about you?"

Ruby didn't answer immediately. When Hildy and she had run away in June, Ruby had not told her grandmother. She'd just left a note, because she had wanted to avoid a scene with the old woman.

Finally, Ruby shrugged. "Who knows? But I'm more concerned with how she takes to muh daddy. Will she let him in the house or run him off like an ol' stray dawg?"

Nate Konning was the son-in-law she'd never met. Her only surviving daughter, Beulah, had met Nate at a Texas camp meeting, married him, then returned alone to the Ozarks after they broke up. Nate hadn't known that his wife was expecting a child at the time. When Beulah died, she left Grandma Skaggs angry at Nate and bitter at having to raise a tomboy granddaughter.

Earlier, Ruby and Nate had decided that if worse came to worse, they'd go to Seth and Rachel Highton's. The cousins had met Seth when they ran away in June, and later met Rachel, whom he had just married. Their place was within walking distance of Possum Hollow.

At midmorning the next day the train arrived in St. Louis. Hildy helped the two young Farnham children leave the train,

while Nate, Matthew Farnham, and the conductor assisted Mrs.
Farnham off. A porter got the wheelchair for Ruby just as Mrs.
Farnham's parents drove up in a big Cadillac sedan.

Mrs. Farnham greeted her parents, who were obviously concerned over the condition of their crippled daughter. She'd con-
tracted polio since they'd last seen one another. Mrs. Farnham
assured her parents that she was fine.

Hildy liked Mr. and Mrs. Sherman at once. He was a haber-
dasher by trade, a dealer in men's clothing and accessories. He
was quite bald, thickening around the middle, and already per-
spiring in the morning humidity.

His wife was stout and gray. She gushed happily at the sight
of her daughter and grandchildren. Hildy found herself smiling
at the reunion. Then the smile faded as she wondered if her own
grandmother would show her the same kind of welcome in the
Ozarks.

After everyone was introduced, Mr. Sherman announced a
surprise for Hildy, Ruby, and her father.

"A salesman who calls regularly on me, name of Nevin Parnell, says he's heading to Little Rock on business. Said that since
I'm such a good customer, he'd be happy to drop you three off
in the Ozarks. He's standing over there by his car."

Hildy looked at the man, of medium height with dark brown
hair and eyes, standing beside a big Chrysler sedan.

As Nate Konning gratefully shook Mr. Sherman's hand, Matthew Farnham spoke up, "I'm glad my father-in-law was able
to arrange a ride for you, but getting back here on time is your
own responsibility, Nate. Remember that you need to be here
two days earlier than the girls. They'll ride back to California
with us."

"What's that all about?" Hildy exclaimed.

Nate nodded reassuringly. "I'll tell ye both about it on the
drive to Arkansas."

The news upset Hildy in a way she couldn't explain. If she
and Ruby were to come back with Nate, they'd all have to leave
the Ozarks a couple of days before they'd planned, otherwise
Hildy and Ruby would be alone. And that could be dangerous,

especially if Vester had followed them back. Besides, it'd be hard enough finding one ride back to St. Louis, let alone two.

Hildy and Ruby said goodbye to Mrs. Farnham and her children. Mr. Farnham introduced their driver to them. Nevin Parnell was a man who smiled a lot and spoke with a big, booming voice. "Pleased to meet you," he said, shaking Nate's hand and nodding to the girls. "Here, let me help with those bags."

Nate rode in the front seat with the driver, while the cousins had the back seat with their bags. As the sedan pulled away from the station, Hildy glanced back at the train. It was already starting to move, heading on to Chicago and then to the East Coast.

Nevin glanced at Hildy. "Forget something, little lady?"

She shook her head, glad that there had been no sign of Vester. "No," she said, leaning back in the seat and relaxing for the first time since she thought she'd seen Vester on the train.

"First trip here?" Nevin asked. He was a friendly, talkative man. He steered the car around a milkman's horse and wagon. Nevin waved, and the milkman in his white uniform waved back. Then the man commented, "He's running late. He's usually left quarts of milk on doorsteps all over town long before now."

Ruby pointed through the narrow windshield. "Up yonder— what're them thar—I mean, what're those boys doin'?"

Hildy followed her cousin's pointing finger. A half-block ahead, a husky man hoisted a block of ice over his left shoulder with a pair of huge steel tongs.

"That's the ice man," Nevin explained. "He's carrying that fifty-pound chunk to the icebox in that house on the right. See the sign in the window? Says '50.' That's how he knows what size block of ice to deliver."

The girls' first look at a big city with its unfamiliar ways was soon left far behind. Hildy was relieved when Nevin said he would be returning to St. Louis the following Monday afternoon. Everyone could ride back with him if they were waiting about noon at Possum Hollow's only general store. Hildy didn't think she'd be ready to return by then, but Nate had to, and Ruby would go with him.

Hildy felt a surge of anxiety as dusk crept over the steep wooded Ozarks. *Time's running out*, she thought, *and I'm not even there yet!*

The driver stopped at the top of a ridge at Hildy's instructions. She would walk from there. Ruby volunteered to go with Hildy to face her grandmother, but Hildy shook her head.

"Just wait here a few minutes, please," she said, sliding out onto the rocky ground. "If it's okay, I'll wave from the house, and you can go on."

Hildy carried her new shoes in her left hand and the cardboard suitcase in the other. Barefooted, she started through the gathering gloom toward her grandmother's.

Hildy's throat felt tight as she approached the split-log house from the front. Beyond the small house, she could see the smokehouse, harness shed, barn, outhouse, and what was left of a chicken house.

Against the left side of the house, she caught a glimpse of the familiar wooden bench with the blue granite pan for washing up. Hildy couldn't see the well and cistern that were located at the back of the house, but she remembered them.

Her heart gave a leap and she swallowed hard, remembering the last time she and Ruby had been at that well. Just as they'd raised the lard pail with the hard-as-a-rock homemade butter from where it was kept cool in the deep well, Vester had shown up.

Hildy shuddered, remembering the sight of the vulgar man chewing on an apple, the juice running down the corner of his mouth and into his beard.

Well, Hildy thought to herself with relief, *at least I've only got Granny to deal with now.*

She continued down the long path to the house, her heart beating faster and faster. *Just like the last time*, Hildy thought. *She's lit the lamp. I smell the wood stove and cornbread baking.*

Hildy glanced around quickly, remembering Granny's last dog had died and wondering if she had another, but no hound could be seen or heard.

About thirty feet from the front door, Hildy stopped and

raised her voice. "Granny! Granny, it's me, Hildy!"

There was no answer, so she called again, a little louder.

Hildy felt an anxious twinge when there was still no answer. *Maybe she's sick! No, she wouldn't be baking cornbread if she were sick. Maybe she just can't hear me!*

The girl moved closer, her calloused feet hardly feeling the rocky ground. The sagging screen door squeaked open, and a coal-oil lamp was held high in the old woman's left hand. Hildy was about to speak, then stopped in shocked surprise. Her eye caught the light's reflection on the double-barrel of a shotgun in Granny's right hand.

"Scat!" the old woman called harshly. "Git off'n muh prop'ty afore I start blastin'!"

CHAPTER
SEVEN
——

GRANNY'S PLACE

Hildy was so startled she couldn't move. She stood stock still, staring through the gathering dusk at her grandmother.

The silence seemed to upset Granny Dunnigan. She shouted, "I warned ye!" and bent to place the kerosene lamp on the floor just inside the door. In slow, jerky movements, she straightened and lifted the heavy shotgun.

"Granny!" the girl shrieked. "It's me! Hildy!"

Slowly, the old woman lowered the gun. She cocked her head sideways and peered questioningly toward the voice. "Hildy?" she asked warily.

"Yes!" Her relieved cry almost exploded from her mouth. "Hildy Corrigan!"

The old woman still seemed doubtful. "Come closer."

Hildy obliged, unsure of whether or not the request was a good sign. As she approached the sagging front porch, Granny stooped and picked up the lamp. She held it in her left hand, extended toward the girl.

Hildy decided she'd better keep talking. "How are you, Granny?" she asked.

The old woman didn't reply, but thrust her head forward in order to better see in the near-darkness. Her sharp, dark eyes peered over the top of her tiny, wire-rimmed glasses. By the lamplight, Hildy could see that her grandmother hadn't changed much since she'd last seen her in June.

More than sixty years of hard work and bitter disappointment had plowed deep furrows in Granny's face. Her shoulders were humped, and her stern looks were exaggerated by a pouty mouth. Her mousy hair, streaked with gray, was parted in the middle and tied in a bun at the back of her neck.

A loose-fitting dress hung limply from her thin shoulders to the tops of her old shoes. Small holes had been cut in her shoes to allow her little toes to stick out. Hildy remembered Granny had told her it eased the pressure of bunions and corns.

"Granny," Hildy began anxiously as she stopped at the top step. "I'm sorry for running away in June. I wrote you, but you didn't answer, so I came to—"

"Hesh up!" her grandmother interrupted. "Come in out o' the night air afore the skeeters carry ye off."

Hildy decided the comment was meant to be friendly, and she followed her grandmother inside. A quick glance around revealed nothing much had changed in the one-room house. It smelled of cornbread and the homegrown tobacco Granny smoked in her corncob pipe. Newspaper had been used for wallpaper. There was a curtained area off in the corner where the old woman slept. A table stood in the middle of the room, an ancient hickory rocking chair nearby, faced by two homemade cane-bottom chairs. Grandpa Dunnigan had made all the furniture. The lean-to kitchen was at the far end. The loft where Hildy had slept was overhead.

Granny stood the gun in a corner behind the door and carried the lamp to the kitchen table. "Where's Vester?" she asked, turning around to face Hildy.

"I don't know."

Granny blinked in surprise. "He didn't fetch ye?"

Hildy shook her head, feeling somewhat frightened. Granny's question confirmed her involvement in Vester's actions.

"I came on my own—just to apologize," Hildy said.

"Ye came clear across the country from Californy, all by yore-self, jist to do that?"

"And to help you understand that my place is with my family in California, no matter how much I love you."

Hildy was about to explain that Ruby and Uncle Nate were waiting for her at the top of the hill, when Granny took a couple of shuffling steps closer. She studied Hildy, her eyes narrowed into slits. Slowly, she stretched out an age-spotted hand and lightly touched Hildy's arm. "Set a spell," she said.

Hildy had secretly hoped to be greeted with a warm hug and maybe even a kiss on the cheek, but she also knew that Granny wasn't the hugging kind. The light tap on her arm was about the closest sign of welcome Granny would give.

"Uh—" Hildy hesitated, then added quickly, "Ruby's outside with—"

"Ruby!" Granny spat the name out as though it were something bad in her mouth. "That woodscolt!"

Hildy pleaded, "Please don't call her that! We found her father. He's with her now in the car."

"Her *father*?" Granny blurted, her voice cracking with disbelief. "She ain't got no pa!"

Hildy shook her head vigorously, her long brown braids flying. "Yes, she has! We found him. He and Ruby are on their way to see Ruby's grandmother, but I'd like you to meet—"

At the mention of her own sister, Granny interrupted. "That sharp-tongued ol' biddy won't cotton to him a-tall! And it ain't likely Gussie'll welcome Ruby, neither. I heard how she run off with ye, leavin' jist a note."

Hildy stirred uneasily, sensing her grandmother's rising emotions about her older sister.

"Is it okay if I stay the night?" Hildy asked. "If so, I've got to tell Ruby and Uncle Nate and the driver so they can go on to Grandma Skaggs'. But if it's not okay to stay here, I'll just go with them."

Granny eased into her hickory rocking chair. It was nearly as old as she was. " 'Course ye kin stay! Ye run tell them folks t' git on. Then I'd be obliged if'n ye went to the well and fetched the milk. Cornbread's purdy near ready. After supper, we'uns kin talk."

Hildy smiled. "Thanks, Granny!" The girl whirled and ran barefooted into the night air. The moment she'd opened the front door, the Chrysler's lights came on. Hildy followed them as she ran up the stony drive.

"It's okay, it's okay," she called. When they hesitated, she ran up to the car and stuck her head in the passenger's side. "I'm going to stay. Thanks for the ride, Mr. Nevin. Ruby, Uncle Nate, I hope things go well for you when you get to Grandma Skaggs' place."

"Me, too," Ruby said wistfully. "But if'n they don't, and she kicks us out, we'll go to Seth and Rachel's. Either way, let's meet tomorrow mornin' at Mr. Galvin's general store."

Hildy nodded and hurried down the hill with a silent prayer. The big Chrysler vanished into the night.

Hildy was so familiar with Granny's place that even in the darkness she went straight to the well. She drew the bucket of milk up on the long rope. Milk meant Granny still kept a cow. Hildy carried the pail into the house.

"Feels good to be here, Granny," Hildy said, following the wonderful cornbread fragrance across the plank floor to the lean-to kitchen.

Granny used a scorched and ragged potholder to remove a pan of cornbread from the oven of the wood-burning stove. "It's yore home, Hildy."

Hildy didn't answer for a moment. She followed her grandmother back into the room, where the cornbread was placed on a trivet at the table.

"It's sort of my second home," Hildy said, "my home when I'm away from the rest of my family."

Granny looked up with dark eyes that seemed to snap. "Yo're the only family I got, Hildy."

"You have your sister," the girl said gently.

Granny snorted. "Gussie ain't nothin' to me! 'Sides, she dips snuff!"

Hildy wanted to ask how that was different from Granny smoking a pipe, but decided against it. Instead, she turned to the small cupboard and began removing dishes before asking, "What happened between you two, anyway?"

"She done me wrong, that's what happened!"

Hildy began setting the table. "How?"

Granny walked over to the bucket of water sitting on a small dropleaf table opposite the cupboard. "I don't want to talk about it." She lifted the long-handled dipper and started to fill two glasses, then stopped. "Reckon we don't need water an' milk both," she said.

Hildy took a slow, deep breath, then risked another question that might upset her grandmother. "You two ever going to make up?"

Granny sat down at the table and motioned for Hildy to do the same. "Not 'less'n she done says she's sorry first."

There was such a determined edge to the old woman's voice that Hildy decided not to pursue the matter.

Granny dropped her head and muttered quickly, "Lord, for this which we are about to receive, we thank Ye. Amen." She raised her head. "Pass the cornbread."

Hildy passed the bread, thinking about how Granny's religious beliefs were never allowed to interfere with her strong opinions.

During the simple meal, Hildy waited for Granny to ask about the rest of the Corrigan family. When she didn't, Hildy casually mentioned her father. Granny snorted. She had never liked her son-in-law and still blamed him for the death of her last surviving daughter.

Hildy felt a slow tension start to build inside as she finished telling about everyone from Molly to baby Joey. Granny didn't respond to one mention of a name.

After Hildy had done the dishes and Granny had smoked her corncob pipe of vile-smelling tobacco, Hildy decided she had to make something clear. She set the last dish back in the cupboard while trying to think how to say it tactfully. "You know, Granny, I can only stay a few days. Then I'm going back home."

The woman knocked the ashes from her pipe into an old coffee can before answering. "Ye belong here with me, Hildy."

There was such a firm tone to her words that Hildy again felt a sense of alarm. *Will Granny actually try to keep me from returning to California?* she wondered. This was instantly followed by another, even more unsettling thought, *She could almost do it, if Vester were here!*

Hildy walked across the room and knelt at the side of the hickory rocking chair. She took her grandmother's wrinkled hand and looked into her dark eyes. "Granny, I love you, but I'm going back home in a few days. I just came to ask your forgiveness for running off in June, and I hope you understand that my place is there, with my family."

"Suppose'n I won't forgive ye?"

Hildy took her time before answering. "I've done all I can, coming across country to personally ask you. If you don't, it'll hurt me terribly, but I really think it'll hurt you more, Granny. And I wouldn't want that."

Granny didn't answer, but changed the subject. "Been a turrible bad summer," she said. "Not enough rain. Woods are bone dry, so ye be keerful if'n ye go a-walkin'. Don't make no sparks or nothin' to cause a fahr."

"I'll be careful," Hildy said, and asked about things in Possum Hollow.

Promptly at nine o'clock, Granny announced it was bedtime. Hildy climbed the loft to the corded bed. She undressed and eased onto the sweet-smelling straw tick and goose-down pillow. Granny blew out the lamp below, and the old house was cast in total darkness.

Hildy said her prayers. Her lips moved but no words escaped her mouth. She prayed for Ruby and her father, and wondered what kind of a reception they'd received at Gussie Skaggs'.

Finally, Hildy dealt with her own growing concern. "Lord, please let Granny say she forgives me. Help her to make up with her sister. And don't let Granny try to keep me here when it's time to go home."

The next morning, Hildy helped with the milking while

Granny threw grain to the chickens running loose in the barn-yard. Hildy sat down on Granny's three-legged stool and held the bucket between her legs.

"Granny," she asked, "How come a cow is always milked from the right and a horse is mounted from the left?"

The old woman smiled wanly for the first time since Hildy's return. "Ain't no reason I know of," she said. "Jist hurry and finish so's we kin have breakfust. I saved me a piece of ham from the smokehouse for when ye come home."

Hildy was disturbed by Granny's reference again to this being her home, but she said nothing. She milked as fast as she could, the sound of milk squirting into the metallic bottom of the bucket changing to the soft slushing of the pail being filled.

At breakfast Granny skimmed the foam off the fresh milk and lightly sprinkled it with sugar. "Jist the way ye like it, Hildy," she said, setting it at her granddaughter's place.

Hildy ate with contentment the warm, sweetened foam with the smoked ham, biscuits and country gravy. Between bites, she asked if her grandmother would like to walk into town with her so she could meet Ruby and her father.

Granny declined, saying, "Cain't walk much no more."

After the dishes were done, Hildy started out barefooted along the familiar rocky and rutted road toward town. She was passing the one-room schoolhouse where she'd attended when she heard laughter. She looked up, remembering that mocking sound.

"Look who's here!" Bertha Killian exclaimed, throwing down a baseball bat. "It's Hildy Corrigan! Hey, Hildy, where's that no-account cousin of yores?"

Hildy noticed at once that "Big Bertha" had grown even more during the summer. She was much taller than Ruby or herself. Her body seemed to be more muscular from her shoulders down, without a noticeable waist or knees.

Without answering the question about her cousin, Hildy turned her gaze to Iris Hastings, who had been pitching the ball to Bertha. Iris was much smaller, but every bit as much a bully.

Then Hildy saw who the other person on the schoolground

was. Elston Edwards was playing outfield. He was solid as a snubbing post with mean little brown eyes and a shock of un-combed hair. He had always boasted there wasn't a boy in Possum Hollow he couldn't whip. He had warned Ruby that he'd do the same to her if she weren't a girl. Ruby had always yelled, "Ye jist try it, and ye'll be plumb sorry!"

Iris echoed her friend's question. "Yeah! Where's Ruby?"

"At her grandmother's, I guess," Hildy answered.

Elston's dirt-streaked face split into a tormenting grin. "You guess? Don't you know?"

Hildy had kept walking, hoping to avoid trouble.

"Answer me!" Bertha yelled, stalking toward Hildy, "Or do ye want me to make ye?"

Hildy started to explain, but stopped when a challenge came from behind her.

"I'll answer for her," Ruby said, stepping out of the woods. She climbed over a split-rail fence at the end of the schoolyard.

Hildy was surprised at Ruby's sudden appearance, but at the same time, greatly relieved. Her blonde hair was still short but neatly combed, and she wore a plain yellow cotton dress. She walked a little stiffly toward the three tormentors, obviously prepared to do whatever was necessary to remind them she was not a person with whom one could trifle.

"Well?" Ruby challenged.

Bertha hunched her shoulders and glowered at Ruby. "Yo're asking for it!" she cried, waddling toward Ruby.

Elston reached out a big hand and stopped her as she passed him. "Now, hold on, Bertha!"

The big girl frowned. "Why?"

" 'Cause I said so!" Elston replied a little sharply, but his eyes never left Ruby.

Hildy was startled, then remembered that Elston had never seen Ruby in a dress or with her hair longer than the boyish bob she'd always worn.

Then Ruby seemed to remember what she'd told Hildy in California, because her manner suddenly changed.

"Elston?" Ruby asked with a smile that would have dazzled any boy. "Is that you?"

"It's me." The boy approached Ruby with a wide grin.

Hildy was relieved, then glanced at Bertha's face. It was black as a tornado. She scowled at both Ruby and Elston.

"Oh-oh!" Hildy whispered to herself. "Now what?"

Chapter Eight

A TROUBLED FAMILY REUNION

Ruby seemed to sense Hildy's concern, for she shot a quick look in Hildy's direction and smiled reassuringly. Then Ruby turned again to widen her smile at Elston as he hurried to meet her.

He said, "You've changed a powerful lot, Ruby!"

"I have?" she asked so innocently that Hildy almost giggled.

Bertha overheard and yelled, "Lettin' yore hair grow didn't help yore looks none!"

Ruby spun to face Bertha, but Elston grabbed Ruby's arm. "Hold on, now!" he said quietly. "I'll take care of this!" He turned back to Bertha. "You and Iris go play by yourselves."

"We need ye to shag fly balls," Bertha protested.

Elston didn't even look around, but kept smiling and talking to Ruby.

Hildy saw Bertha puff up as though she were about to burst. The big girl thumped the bat against her left palm but made no move to leave. Iris whispered something, and Bertha scowled at Ruby.

At the same instant, Hildy saw Ruby's father walking down the road. Hildy hurried toward him, calling, "Hi, Uncle Nate!" She desperately wanted to know how Grandma Skaggs had reacted last night, but it was more important to quickly explain the situation on the schoolyard.

When she had done that, her uncle nodded in understanding. He hurried toward Bertha and Iris, with Hildy following a step behind. Bertha and Iris stepped back. Nate nodded to them but walked up to his daughter and the boy.

"Howdy," he said, offering his right hand to Elston. "I'm Ruby's father, Nate Konning."

Elston blinked in surprise as he shook hands. Then he glanced at Ruby. "He is?"

"Shore is!" Ruby replied. "Daddy, this here's Elston. That's Bertha over thar with the bat, and Iris with her."

"Ruby, he ain't yore daddy!" Bertha called. "Yo're a woods-colt!"

A flush of anger reddened Ruby's cheeks, then she forced a smile. "That's where yo're wrong, Bertha! He's really muh Daddy. I'd explain how we found each other, but yo're not smart enough to understand."

"Now, Ruby!" her father said reprovingly.

Hildy saw Bertha take two quick steps toward Ruby, then stop uncertainly, looking at Nate.

"Come on, Iris," the big girl growled, turning away.

Hildy sighed with relief as Bertha and Iris hurried across the schoolyard and disappeared up the mountain.

Hildy turned back to her cousin, her uncle, and Elston.

The boy asked Ruby, "You back to stay?"

Ruby shook her head so the growing blonde hair rippled in soft, gentle waves. "No. We'll be jist a few days. Come to see muh grandma and let her'n muh daddy git acquainted. Then we'll be a-headin' back to Californy."

"Too bad!" Elston said. He looked up at Nate and asked, "What do you do for a livin', Mr. Konning?"

Hildy involuntarily sucked in her breath. Ruby didn't like being a preacher's kid, although she'd recently come to accept her father's calling. But Hildy wasn't sure what Ruby would say about that to people here in the Ozarks.

Ruby surprised Hildy by explaining, "Daddy was a Texas cowboy, but he's a-gonna be a preacher man."

"You don't say!" Elston took a step backward, as though he didn't want to be too close to such a person.

Nate nodded. "I had the call to preach a powerful long time ago. But I didn't answer till after I found God had done given me a daughter an' turned my life around. I'm right proud to be her pa and to preach the gospel."

Hildy watched Elston shift uncomfortably from one dirty brown bare foot to another. Then he seemed to come to terms with Ruby having a father called to preach.

"Mr. Konning," Elston exclaimed, "you should meet Iris' grandpappy, Rufus Hurley. He's the only preacher hereabouts. Leastwise, he was till he took sick. Heart." The boy somberly tapped his chest. "Ain't preached a lick since. He's powerful old. Iris said he's talking of closing the church."

"I'm mighty sorry to hear that," Nate replied.

"Say!" Elston snapped his fingers and looked up at Nate. "Maybe you could preach for him this Sunday. Iris said a while ago her grandpappy allowed as how nobody around these parts can do that. But maybe you could."

Hildy watched her uncle as he considered the unexpected development. Then he nodded, "I'd be obliged if ye'd introduce me to him."

"Do it right now!" Elston cried. "Come on!" He turned to Ruby and smiled again. "Why don't you walk along? You'n me can visit while Brother Rufus and your pa talk. Hildy, you can come too, if you've a mind to."

Hildy wanted to protest, because she was bursting with curiosity about the kind of reception Ruby and her father had received last night at Grandma Skaggs'.

Ruby seemed to sense that, for she turned around and looked at her cousin. "Maybe later, Elston." Ruby said. "Me'n Hildy got to talk now."

Hildy was pleased, but she could see that Elston was not.

Still, he nodded, grinned at Ruby, then led Nate Konning down the road toward town. Hildy and Ruby fell into step some distance behind them.

"Well?" Hildy asked eagerly, feeling the rocks on the roadway under her bare feet, "How'd it go last night?"

"You first! How'd yore o'nery ol' granny treat ye?"

"Ruby!" Hildy almost exploded in exasperation.

"Okay, okay! I'll tell ye! Naturally, Grandma started right off, bawlin' me out for runnin' off with ye an' only leavin' a note." Ruby paused, smiling in remembrance. "Then Grandma's eyes got big as saucers when I said, 'This here's muh daddy.' "

"Then what happened?"

"At first, Grandma didn't believe it. But when Daddy talked about meeting Beulah at the Texas camp meetin', and getting married and all, well, Grandma allowed as how he was tellin' the truth."

Hildy was dying of anxiety. "But what happened?"

Ruby shrugged. "What'd ye expect? Grandma started in a-blamin' Daddy for Beulah leaving' him an' comin' back to the Ozarks where I was born. Then Grandma got really riled up, sayin' as how it was Daddy's fault her daughter died, leaving Grandma to raise me all alone."

"What'd your father say?"

"He tried to explain, but Grandma wouldn't listen. Then she turned right around an' said she was too much of a Christian lady to put a dawg out at night without no place to stay. So I could sleep in the house, but Daddy'd have to sleep in the barn. She said I could come back, but for muh daddy to never darken her door again."

"Oh, Ruby!" Hildy reached out and gripped her cousin's arms. "I'm so sorry!"

"Cain't be he'ped. Grandma's as hardheaded as her o'nery ol' sister. Them two's a caution, ain't they?"

"What're you going to do?"

"Reckon Daddy an' me'll walk over to Seth and Rachel's place an' stay till it's time to go back to St. Louis."

The girls had met Seth and Rachel Highton in June, when

they were disguised as boys trying to find Hildy's family and escape Vester. The memory of the Hightons' kindness also reminded Hildy that Spud had been with them then. On their journey west, the girls had met Spud, a runaway boy whom Hildy had recently talked into going back to New York to try to reconcile with his hot-tempered father. Hildy always felt a little funny inside when she thought of the freckle-faced boy with the green eyes.

Ruby was saying, "I shore ain't gonna stay no place where muh daddy ain't welcome! Now, tell me about what yore Granny done last night."

Hildy told all that had been said and done at Granny Dunnigan's. Hildy was just finishing her report when she turned at the jingling sound of chains and creaking of harness leather.

The cousins stepped out of the unpaved road into the brush to let a wagon and two mules pass. Two hounds trotted at the rear of the wagon. Then Hildy recognized the driver.

Sam Nayton lived near the house Hildy and her family had rented until June. He wore his usual blue overalls with one strap fastened. His right cheek bulged with a wad of chewing tobacco.

"Well, now!" he drawled, hauling back on the reins. "I heard tell ye was back!"

Hildy watched the man's two hounds. They flopped down in the shade of the wagon. Usually the bluetick and the redbone ran at her, baying and threatening to eat her alive.

"Hello, Mr. Nayton," Hildy greeted him.

Ruby asked politely, "How's yore missus?"

Hildy remembered that Mrs. Nayton was a sharp-tongued woman so crippled with arthritis that she couldn't leave her chair. But she enjoyed gossip, which she gleaned from people who stopped by the Nayton's log house. Neither Hildy nor Ruby liked the woman, because she enjoyed other people's hurts. Hildy knew that the bitter woman had especially enjoyed Ruby's reputation for being fatherless. Maybe that was why Ruby was politely inquiring about Mrs. Nayton. Ruby had news that would set her back on her heels.

"Tolerable," the man replied to Ruby's question. "She'll be

glad I run into y'all. She cain't hardly believe ye found yore pa, Ruby."

Hildy blinked in surprise, then frowned. She wondered, *How's he already know about Ruby finding her father?*

But before she could ask, Ruby smiled happily. "She's one o' the people I been a-thinkin' about since we found him. I'd be obliged if'n ye told her I'd be proud to bring him by so she kin see him with her very own eyes."

Hildy suppressed a knowing smile. It was Ruby's way of making Ozark people "eat crow" because she really did have a father.

"Much obliged, Ruby," the man said, clucking to the team. "Come by anytime. The missus'll likely talk yore arm off, 'cause she don't git out much. Makes up for it when company comes."

Hildy watched the team move on toward town with the rattling of chains and crunch of iron wheels.

Ruby let out a little laugh. "He acts like his poor crotchety ol' wife never said a mean thing to me! Why, I remember when you'n me went to his place las' June, a-lookin' for Molly an' the kids, and even Mr. Nayton said spiteful things! They hurt, but I'm a-gettin' even, showin' off muh daddy!"

Hildy frowned. "Wish I'd asked how he'd heard about your father so quickly." She shrugged, then changed the subject. "Wonder if Iris' grandfather really will ask your father to preach next Sunday?"

"Reckon we'll know soon enough. Come on, let's go see who else we can find so's I can show 'em I really do have me a daddy."

"I'd rather go see your grandmother."

Ruby stopped in the middle of the road and looked up in surprise. "Why's that?"

"Maybe I can talk her into changing her mind about your father."

Ruby threw back her head and laughed. "Ye'd have as much chance o' doin' that as ye would of buildin' a snowman in summertime!"

"Maybe so, but I'd like to try."

For a moment, Ruby studied her cousin in thoughtful silence.

Then Ruby nodded. "Okay! Come on!"

Gussie Skaggs' log house was on the side of a steep hill just beyond the small business section of Possum Hollow. It showed the neglect common to the homes of elderly widows who lived alone in the mountains. The stone chimney had started to pull away from the house. The windows were so dirty, Hildy was sure they hadn't been washed in years.

She and Ruby walked to the back door. Hildy smelled the good, rich fragrance of the smokehouse. Skinny, half-wild, white Leghorn chickens scattered in fright as the girls approached. The fowl were never penned, although they roosted in the chicken house at night.

"Watch out!" Ruby cried suddenly.

Hildy turned around to see that she'd almost walked into a twisted strand of shoulder-high wire running from the back porch. Her eyes followed the wire to where it branched off toward the cistern, well, smokehouse, barn, and outhouse.

Ruby asked, "What do ye reckon all them wahrs is? They was never here before."

"Maybe she can't see well, and follows the wires in winter so she won't get lost in the snow going to the out buildings."

Ruby shrugged as the cousins mounted the creaking, broken back steps to Grandma Skaggs' house. Ruby pushed the door open onto a long screened-in porch.

"Grandma, I'm back!" Ruby called. "With Hildy."

Grandma Skaggs poked her head out of the kitchen door that opened onto the porch. For a moment, Hildy thought it was her own grandmother, because the sisters looked so much alike.

Gussie Skaggs was nearly seventy, Hildy remembered, about five years older than her own grandmother. Ruby's grandmother was grayer than her sister, but wore her hair back in the same severe bun. Grandma Skaggs also wore wire-framed glasses and a perpetual frown.

"Howdy, Hildy," the old woman said, looking over the top of her glasses while drying her withered hands on a blue apron that had seen better days. "Light and sit." She waved toward a rough wooden bench that Hildy knew Grandma Skaggs' husband had made many years ago.

Hildy felt the same twinge of disappointment as she had last night when her own grandmother hadn't greeted her with more than a light touch on the arm. Hildy wondered if Ruby had received any more affection from this stern old woman.

"Thanks," Hildy said, taking a seat at the far end of the bench so there would be room for the others. "You look good," she added, smiling at Mrs. Skaggs.

"Don't do a body no good to complain," she said, picking up an old relic of a fan and vigorously waving it in front of her wrinkled face. "Shore's been a scorcher of a summer! No tornadoes, thank God! But not much rain, neither. Whole country's so dry it's got me plumb scared. Come a lightnin' storm like it does sometimes this time o' year, an' the whole woods'll burst into flame!" She waved at the surrounding wooded mountains.

Hildy nodded. "My grandmother said that too."

"Hepzibah!" Grandma Skaggs almost spat the word at mention of her sister. "She's got a disposition so bad she could turn milk sour with one look!"

"Oh," Hildy said, forcing a smile, "don't say things like that! She's your sister!"

"Ain't no sister o' mine!" Grandma Skaggs fluttered her fan vigorously. "After what she done!"

"What did she do?" Hildy asked.

Ruby's grandmother scowled fiercely at Hildy. "Why, she— she—oh, never ye mind!"

Hildy had the feeling that the two elderly sisters didn't even really remember why they hadn't spoken for all these years. *Sure wish I could get these two to make up while we're here!* Hildy thought.

The topic of conversation shifted. Grandma Skaggs complained bitterly about the hens not laying, her butchering hog dying, and her garden doing poorly.

Hildy and Ruby tried to talk about other things, especially California and finding Nate, but Ruby's grandmother wasn't interested. Finally, the girls excused themselves and went back to meet Nate.

Ruby muttered as they walked down the middle of the dirt road. "She shore is a hard-head! Cain't tell her nothin'! Same's yore granny!"

Hildy sighed, feeling Ruby was right. She glanced up at the sound of trace chains. "There's Mr. Nayton again," she said. "I want to ask him something."

The girls waited until the mules drew up and the driver looked down expectantly. "Y'all want something?" he asked, spitting tobacco into the roadside brush.

"Yes," Hildy said, shading her eyes from the sun and looking up. "I know news travels fast in these hills, Mr. Nayton, but we just got in at dusk last night. So how'd you hear about us so soon?"

"Why, from Vester, o' course."

"Vester?" Hildy and Ruby exclaimed together.

—

Chapter Nine

HILDY OVERHEARS A TERRIBLE THREAT

S am Nayton nodded and spat tobacco juice over the nearest wheel. "Why, shore! Vester Hardesty come by our place this mornin'. He told me' an' muh missus." Nayton slapped the reins. "Giddyup, mules!"

Hildy exclaimed to Ruby, "Then I did see Vester on the train!"

"Ye reckon he's gonna try a-keepin' ye from leavin' here?"

Hildy nodded, feeling her insides tighten in a knot of apprehension. "Not just me. You, too."

Ruby cocked her chin defiantly. "He cain't do that—not whilst muh daddy's around!"

"But your daddy has to leave early, remember? Mr. Farnham wants him back in St. Louis two days before the rest of us have to leave for California."

Ruby groaned. "I plumb forgot that!" She glanced down the road where her father had gone with Elston. "Let's go tell Daddy!"

Hildy shook her head. "I think we should let him finish talking with Iris' grandfather."

"Reckon yo're right. But it won't do no harm to sit on the porch an' wait. Maybe Elston's thar yet."

Hildy didn't catch her cousin's meaning. Instead, Hildy tugged thoughtfully at the end of her long brown braids. "Uh—you can do that if you want, but I think I'd better go talk to Granny."

"What for?"

"I want her to tell Vester there's no such thing as a hex and that she didn't really put one on him."

Ruby snorted. "She ain't likely to do that! She enjoys skeerin' people, 'specially ones like Vester."

"Maybe so, but I have to try. See you later."

Hildy set off in a steady dogtrot along the rocky road, trying to control the anxious feeling in her stomach. When she could, she took a shortcut across a split-rail fence and through the hardwood forest.

She noticed how unusually dry everything was. She remembered that both her Granny and Ruby's grandmother had mentioned the extremely dry summer and lack of rain. All it would take to set the woods on fire was a lightning strike or some careless human to drop a match or let a trash fire get away.

But Hildy's mind soon focused on what she should say to Granny about Vester. "Lord, help me to say the right thing," the girl prayed aloud, puffing from the exertion of climbing.

Her heart beat hard and she was breathing rapidly when she topped the last ridge and saw the familiar log house below in a clearing. Hildy also saw something else and jumped behind a slippery elm. She flattened herself there and slowly peered around the trunk.

Vester Hardesty stood at the back door, hat in hand, speaking to Granny Dunnigan. She had not opened the screen door, but was talking through it. Hildy could hear the old woman's voice, high and shrill, but could not make out the words.

I've got to get closer! she thought, and began slipping quickly and quietly from one brush or tree to another. She kept an eye out for Vester's hound so it wouldn't betray her presence, but she didn't see any dog.

Hildy came to the last tree before the clearing around her grandmother's property. The smokehouse was the nearest building from the forest, but a good thirty yards of open space stretched between the two shelters. For a moment, Hildy hesitated, thinking how to get closer without being seen.

Hildy decided. *If I go any other direction, Vester'll probably see me, because he's a hunter and looks for movement. So I'd better come up behind him, facing Granny. She won't see me because of her poor eyesight.*

Taking a deep breath, the girl dashed silently across the open space. She darted behind the smokehouse and stopped, trying to control the sound of her ragged breathing.

I feel terrible sneaking around like this, she thought, *but I've got to hear what they're saying.*

Hildy leaned hard against the back side of the smokehouse. Carefully, she peeked around the corner.

Vester had turned slightly to one side so Hildy could see his hands. With one, he was nervously clutching a rabbit's foot. The good-luck charm dangled from the bib of his patched and faded blue-denim overalls. In his other hand, he held the black slouch hat against his leg. Hildy thought she could detect nervous perspiration on Vester's pockmarked forehead.

But his voice didn't show any fear, "Now lookee here, ol' woman!" he cried with anger. "Far's I'm concerned, I went to Californy and brought yore granddaughter back. So I kept muh end o' the bargain! Now ye keep yores!"

Hildy jerked her head back suddenly, feeling sick inside. *So Granny did send him to get me!* she thought with dismay. Then her pain changed to anger. *I should have known! She'll never change! Granny lied to Molly and betrayed me last June! All she thinks about is herself!*

Then Hildy sighed, thinking, *But she's my grandmother, and I love her!*

She heard Granny's sharp answer to Vester. "I told ye, Hildy's come back on her own! Ye didn't have nothin' to do with it!"

"Ye sayin' ye won't take the hex off'n me?"

"Why should I?"

Hildy eased her head around the corner to see Vester's pock-marked face turn dark with anger. He shouted, "Listen, ye ol' granny woman! If'n ye don't take it off'n me right now, yo're gonna be plumb sorry!"

"Are ye threatenin' me?" Granny demanded, her voice hard and brittle as an ice pond straining under too much weight.

"Call it what ye want!" Vester snapped, his voice rising. "Now, what's it a-gonna be?"

Hildy held her breath while Granny considered the heavyset man through sharp, dark eyes. When the old woman spoke again, her tone softened.

"Tell ye what, Vester," she began, thoughtfully caressing her chin. "Ye make shore Hildy stays with me, an' I'll take the spell off."

Hildy stifled a pained gasp. *I can't believe it!* her mind screamed.

Vester shook his head so hard the long, untidy hair whipped around his neck. "I done muh part gittin' her here. It's yore job to keep her."

"Yore job's whatever I say it is!" Granny's tone carried anger. "An' I'm a-sayin' y'all got to see she don't leave here 'less'n I give the word! Ye hear?"

"I hear ye."

"Good!"

"Then take the hex off o' me this instant."

"Don't tell me what to do, Vester!"

Hildy heard him reply calmly but with a deadly edge to his words, as though he'd just become sure of something. "Listen, ye old witch! I remember what ye said when I set out to Cali-forny. Ye said the hex lasts until Hildy's back here, or yo're dead. Now, if'n ye fell in the well or somethin'—"

Granny interrupted with a screech. She kicked the screen door open with her foot and yelled in his face, "Ye so much as try to harm a hair o' muh head, Vester Hardesty—"

"Ah, hesh up!" Vester broke in. "I'll keep both them gals here, 'cause I got muh own grudge to settle with 'em. But ye'd better take the hex off'n me now, or—"

"I'll take it off when I'm good an' ready!" Granny snapped, her voice still shrill. "An' don't go takin' yore grudge out on Hildy! I don't care about her woodscolt cousin, but don't ye touch muh Hildy!"

"I'll do what I please, ol' woman, 'cause ye cain't hurt me if'n yo're dead! The hex'll be gone with ye! So ye cain't skeer me no more! I done warned ye!"

As the bearded mountaineer turned from Granny, Hildy jerked her head back so she was completely hidden by the smokehouse.

She heard Vester's heavy boots as he stomped angrily across the yard, scattering the half-wild chickens in every direction. Granny called something after him, but Hildy didn't catch the words.

She remained perfectly still, her body pressed tightly against the boards, her heart thudding so hard it hurt her chest.

Her thoughts exploded. *He threatened Granny's life! And he wants revenge on Ruby and me for getting him arrested after he kidnapped us in June. So even if I stay here, Ruby and I are both in danger!*

Hildy waited in turmoil, giving Vester time to disappear into the woods and Granny time to be back inside. The girl's mind whirled at the terrible, unexpected turn of events.

What'll I do? Hildy asked herself. It was an anguished question torn from the depths of her being.

She realized the great need Granny had for someone young and healthy to help her. But the same was true of her sister, Ruby's grandmother. Hildy thought of the long wires running from Grandma Skaggs' house to the well and various outbuildings. Grandma Skaggs' eyesight was obviously worse than Granny's.

Hildy shuddered in spite of the warm, muggy day, knowing Granny was growing older every day, and she was so terribly alone. Her eyes probably would also fail, and eventually she could be blind. Hildy imagined Granny trying to build a fire in the stove and cook her food without getting burned.

Hildy was aware of a lump in her throat. She tried to swallow, but the lump remained. So did the sick feeling in her stomach.

Another unpleasant image leaped unbidden to the girl's mind. She saw Granny's aching feet shuffling more and more each day. Hildy had noticed the way things slipped out of Granny's hands, showing her arthritis was getting worse. Hildy squeezed her eyes shut, trying to block out the awful vision of Granny falling, all alone, with nobody to help her. With her arthritic hands, she couldn't get up.

Even if Vester didn't carry out his threat to Granny's life, Hildy knew that someday her grandmother would die. She'd probably be all alone in this remote mountain log house, and nobody would know or care.

Eventually, someone would find her body. Hildy's mind pictured her Granny's open coffin in the small log house. The glass-enclosed hearse with four black horses stood waiting to carry the body to the churchyard cemetery. There were only a few mourners, because Granny didn't have many friends. Her tongue was too sharp and her temper too quick.

Of course, her sister wasn't there. Even in death Ruby's grandmother wouldn't forgive Granny. And, Hildy knew, if it was the other way around, Granny wouldn't attend her sister's funeral, either.

Stop it! Hildy scolded herself, opening her eyes. *Even though she's schemed against me, I have to try to think of some way to help Granny. I can't let Vester carry out his threat to harm her and to get even with Ruby and me. But how? What can I do?*

Hildy decided she first needed to talk to Ruby and Uncle Nate. Hildy slipped away toward the woods, keeping the smokehouse between herself and the log house even though Granny probably couldn't see that far.

As the girl's feet turned toward town again, her mind twisted and turned with self-doubt. *She'll be okay if I stay and live with her, but what about my family? Dad? Molly? Elizabeth, Martha, Sarah, Iola, and baby Joey? I promised them a "forever home" where we'll all be together and never have to move again. I've got to make Granny understand my place is with them. But how can I make her believe that when I'd be leaving her all alone, especially since Vester threatened her? And Ruby and me?*

Hildy cut through the woods, barely hearing a squirrel scolding her for trespassing. Instead, another problem came to mind. Hildy remembered her father's words about possibly losing his job and moving from the barn-house when she got back from the Ozarks.

I hope we don't have to move far away again! Hildy thought to herself. *I hope his work is close by so Ruby and I can go to Lone River School! I don't think I could stand it if we moved to Oregon or back to Texas or someplace!*

When she reached Possum Hollow again, Hildy felt as winded and tired as an old hound dog that had run all night.

Still at a short distance, Hildy saw Ruby sitting on the front porch of the home of Iris' grandfather. Elston sat beside Ruby, smiling at her. Ruby was smiling too, but her eyes were lowered, and Hildy heard her cousin giggle.

Ruby had always been a tomboy and never shown any interest in boys, but Hildy realized, *She's flirting with him!*

The front door opened, and Nate Konning stepped out. He turned, reached back inside and shook hands. "Much obliged, Brother Rufus," he said. "I'll try to give them folks a good sermon on the Lord's Day. Now, I'm a-gonna go to the church an' check it out. Y'all hurry an' get well."

Hildy suffered silently while Ruby shyly said goodbye to Elston. Hildy waved to the boy, then fell into step with her uncle and cousin. Hildy wanted desperately to talk about the threat she'd overheard Vester make against herself, Ruby, and Granny. But Ruby babbled on about Elston not being such a bad boy as she had always thought, and Nate was trying to explain the preparations he'd have to make to deliver a sermon on Sunday.

Finally, Hildy couldn't stand it any longer. She took a quick step ahead, whirled in the road and blurted, "Granny's in danger! Vester threatened her! Ruby and me, too! Granny and Vester aren't going to let either of us return to California."

That got Ruby and Nate's attention. They listened silently while Hildy repeated what she'd overheard at her grandmother's place. "I don't know what to do!" she said finally.

Ruby scoffed, "Don't pay no mind to that Vester! He was jist a-blowin' smoke, tryin' to skeer yore granny."

Nate shook his head. "I'm not sure I agree with ye, honey. Let's think a spell on this."

They walked and talked, offering suggestions and ideas until they neared the town's tiny church with its adjacent cemetery.

They were still talking as they pushed through the rusted iron gate into the churchyard. The ground was packed down from the trampling of generations of human feet, countless horses' hooves, innumerable iron-rimmed wagon wheels and hard, rubber-tired buggy wheels.

Hildy hadn't been able to think what she could do to get out of the problems she faced as she, Ruby, and Nate approached the church.

Nate stopped and looked down at her. "Hildy, they's only one thing for ye to do."

"What's that?" she asked eagerly.

"Let's go inside, and I'll tell ye."

He unlocked the door, and Hildy hurried inside, anxious to know what solution her uncle had to offer.

CHAPTER
TEN

—

TROUBLE AND MORE TROUBLE

Hildy glanced around, letting her eyes become accustomed to the dim interior of the small church. She counted about a dozen homemade pews down the middle of the tiny sanctuary with aisles on both sides. A small altar was placed before the front row of pews. There was no room for a choir loft under the plain wooden cross suspended behind the pulpit.

Hildy took a deep breath, feeling the peace she associated with God's presence. But her mind was still on the terrible words she'd overheard between her grandmother and Vester. Hildy turned to look up at her tall uncle. "You were saying there's only one thing for me to do," she prompted.

Nate Konning nodded somberly. "I don't reckon that Vester'll try anything as long as y'all are with me. So it appears like the only smart thing to do is for both Ruby and ye to come back to St. Louis with me when I go."

Hildy shook her head. "I don't want to leave until I've done what I came to do."

She lifted her fingers as she named the reasons. "First, I

wanted Granny's forgiveness for running off last June. Next, I
wanted her to understand my place is with my family. Now I
want to protect her from Vester by having her tell him she didn't
put any hex on him. And I want Ruby and me to be safe from
Vester so we can go home again." She hesitated. "And I'd also
like to know Granny's got someone to look after her."

"They ain't time enough to even begin doin' all them things
in a month o' Sundays," Ruby declared.

Her father said thoughtfully, "Hildy, I think ye already done
all ye can. Ye asked, but if she won't forgive nor understand,
that's her choice, not yours. But there's one thing ye can do."

"What's that?"

"Join me in prayin' about all them problems. Then we should
also invite both yore grandmothers to come to church on Sunday. Maybe the Lord will move on them in a powerful way, an'
things'll happen we couldn't even begin to think about."

Ruby snorted to show her disagreement. "After the way muh
grandmother talked to ye, tellin' ye to never darken her door
again, she's shore not a-gonna come hear ye preach. Besides,
she won't set foot inside a church where her sister is."

Hildy added, "Knowing Granny, if she found out her sister
was going to be there, Granny wouldn't come."

"Well, girls, I believe what the Bible says about the Lord
moving in mysterious ways."

Ruby muttered, "It'd be mysterious alright, an' a miracle if'n
either of 'em showed up at church, let alone both!"

"I agree with you, Ruby. But Uncle Nate's right too. I'll pray
for them to come Sunday."

"Thankee kindly, Hildy." He glanced at Ruby. "How about
it, honey?"

Ruby shrugged and slowly shook her short blonde hair. "I
ain't much on prayin', as ye both know."

Her father nodded but turned back to Hildy. "Let's claim
Matthew 18:19 for both your grandmothers to come."

Hildy frowned. "I don't remember that verse."

"Jesus said, 'Again I say unto you, that if two of you shall agree on earth as touching anything that they shall ask, it shall be done for them. . .' "

"Oh, I like that!" Hildy interrupted. "I'll agree with you on that prayer!"

"One o' my favorites! Now, I'm a-gonna stay here an' pray about that right now, an' what the Lord wants me to say come Sunday. Y'all want to join me?"

Hildy wanted to, but Ruby squirmed uncomfortably, so Hildy decided to go back outside with her. Hildy's eyes were drawn toward the small cemetery next to the church. She started walking toward the fence separating them.

Ruby held back. "Why're ye a-headin' that-away?" Ruby had a superstitious dread of graveyards.

"I was just thinking that someday both our grandmothers are going to be buried here."

"Them two hate each other so much that the first one to go will likely be buried here, but not t'other one!"

"But this is the only cemetery around here."

"Won't matter none to them."

The two girls stopped and looked across the low wooden fence at the crosses and headstones. There were two gates— one at the back near the wooded mountain, and one near the church.

"Sad, isn't it?" Hildy asked.

"Dyin' is always sad."

"I meant it's sad about our grandmothers."

The cousins were silent a moment, looking at the old cemetery. Then Hildy made a decision. "Ruby, I think you'd better go back to St. Louis when your father goes, and I'll stay a little longer."

"What? Leave ye alone here?" Ruby's voice shot up. "Yo're talkin' plumb foolish, Hildy! If'n ye don't go with Daddy an' me, then Vester and yore granny'll never let ye go! Shore, yore daddy'll come for ye when he kin, but he's gonna be powerful mad, and there'd be big trouble! Come back with Daddy and me!"

Hildy knew that her cousin was right, yet the stubborn streak which was both Hildy's weakness and her strength kept her from changing her mind. "I've got to find a way to do what I came to do," she said.

Ruby turned away from the cemetery fence to face the church. "Hildy, look at the facts. First, Granny done ye wrong last June, tellin' lies to Molly and then deceivin' ye. Next, Granny won't forgive ye for takin' off to Californy. Then she told Vester she'd put a hex on him, so he went to fetch ye back. The fact ye came on yore own don't make no never-mind to her. With yore own ears, ye heard her'n Vester a-plannin' on how to keep ye from ever leavin' here!"

"I'll find a way," Hildy said stubbornly.

A little while later the church door opened, and Nate Konning stepped out onto the small porch. He raised his voice. "I'm a-gonna need to rent me a horse and buggy so's I can drive around an' invite people to church. Since it's been closed a while, some folks may not know there's gonna be a service this Lord's Day. You two want to walk along an' he'p me find the livery stable?"

Ruby shook her head. "Ain't no livery stable hereabouts. But sometimes ye kin rent a rig from some farmer for a few days."

Hildy agreed. "Best place to ask is at the general store."

The trio started walking toward the center of Possum Hollow. Ruby updated her father on what Hildy had just said about staying behind.

Nate shook his head in disapproval. "Hildy, your grandmother has a powerful hold on that Vester feller because o' what he believes. She most likely gets a kick out o' havin' such power over him. Now we all know they ain't no such thing as hexes, but sometimes facts don't make no never-mind."

Hildy glanced at Ruby, who had dropped her eyes. Hildy knew her cousin was superstitious. Hildy wasn't quite sure that Ruby believed in hexes, but she certainly was afraid of graveyards because of the "haints." Hildy knew there were no such things as haints or ghosts.

Hildy said, "Maybe I can get Granny to tell Vester she really doesn't have a hex on him."

Ruby clucked her tongue. "Oh, Hildy, Hildy! It jist cain't all be done afore we'uns have to leave!"

"I've got to try," Hildy said firmly. "If I don't, I'd never be able to live with myself."

"Ye got too powerful a conscience," Ruby protested. "I mean, ye felt guilty about us runnin' off last summer when it was yore granny who shoulda been feelin' guilty! Now yo're a-takin' more blame on yoreself. It ain't right, Hildy!"

"I sure do feel guilty," Hildy admitted, "but the only way I know to get over that is to do what I've just told you."

Her uncle said, "I'll pray for ye to do just that."

They approached the sagging wooden overhang above the boardwalk leading to the general store. Two old-timers in ancient overalls and plaid workshirts sat spitting tobacco and whittling sticks on the rickety wooden bench in front of the store window.

Nate spoke to the girls, "Y'all can go on inside. I want to speak to those men an' tell them about Sunday service. I'll join ye inside directly."

The girls nodded and pushed open the door to the store. A small bell announced their entry.

It took Hildy's eyes a moment to adjust from the outside glare to the dim interior. She felt the smooth wooden floor under her feet and could smell the oily sawdust that had been used to sweep it the night before. Her eyes took in the familiar sight of items hanging from the ceiling and walls. Besides the coal-oil lamps mounted in wall brackets, there were horse collars, buggy whips, lanterns, hand tools, and bushel baskets.

"Hildy?" a man's voice asked from behind the high wooden counter. "Ruby? Is it really you?"

"It's us," Ruby answered. "Howdy, Mr. Galvin."

Hildy added her greeting to the merchant. He was as she remembered him—tall and thin, balding with just a patch of blond-gray hair in the middle of his head. He wore a green apron tied at the waist. He had wrapped brown paper to his elbows to keep his white shirtsleeves clean.

"Ruby, I hear you found your father," the merchant said.

"Shore did! He'll be in directly, so ye kin meet him."

"I'd be proud to make his acquaintance, Ruby. Meanwhile, is there anything I can do for either of you?"

The girls shook their heads.

"In that case," the merchant said, "welcome back, and help yourselves to a pickle." He pointed to the open barrel at the end of the counter. "Cut yourselves off a piece of cheese from that wheel and grab a cracker too."

Ruby reached for the long fork and speared a fat pickle. "Don't mind if'n I do. Hildy, ye want one?"

"No, thanks. I'll take a little cheese, though." She picked up a knife and cut a small wedge from the round wheel on the counter, then reached into the open barrel for a soda cracker.

As she enjoyed the first bite, she glanced out the plate glass window in time to see her uncle walking into the middle of the street with one of the old men. Both men's backs were toward Hildy. The old-timer pointed, and Nate walked off in that direction. Hildy guessed he'd been given directions to where he could rent a horse and buggy.

When the door opened, making the bell sound, Hildy turned to face it. Bertha and Iris entered.

Hildy knew instantly that the two girls had seen her and Ruby enter. She also sensed trouble.

Bertha walked straight toward Ruby, who was standing nearer the front door. "Ruby," the large girl began in a hard voice, "now that ye ain't got yore new pa around to protect ye, me'n Iris come to tell ye flat out, ye ain't welcome here! Neither's yore cousin!"

"Yeah!" Iris said, thrusting her chin out.

Hildy saw Ruby drop the remaining piece of pickle on the wooden floor and start toward the two girls, but the merchant was faster.

He hurried from behind the counter and stood between them. "Now, hold on here!" he exclaimed. "I don't want any trouble. Besides, you girls are too big to go around acting like some rowdy boys."

Bertha stood up to the merchant. "Who ye a-callin' big?" she demanded hotly.

The merchant explained evenly, "I meant 'big' like grown-up. And you are—all of you! You're practically young ladies."

"Don't go callin' me no lady!" Bertha flared.

"Yeah!" Iris said.

"Oh, shut up, Iris!" Bertha snapped, whirling on her friend.

Hildy almost smiled in spite of the difficult situation. It was obvious to her that Iris didn't do much thinking for herself, but blindly followed the lead of her friend.

Before anyone could say anything else, the doorbell sounded again. Hildy looked up and sucked her breath in sharply.

Vester Hardesty pushed his way into the store. Hildy wondered if he'd been following them too.

The merchant still stood between the four girls, but turned to look at the new arrival. "Morning, Vester. Haven't seen you in a while."

"Been away," the mountaineer said, glancing first at Hildy and then at Ruby.

"What can I do for you?" Mr. Galvin asked. He gave Ruby, Bertha, and Iris a warning look and walked back behind the counter.

"Gimme a plug o' chawin' tobaccy," Vester replied, still looking at Ruby.

Hildy saw her cousin squirm under the uncouth man's gaze.

"Here you are," the merchant said, reaching into a small cubbyhole and producing an oblong plug of dark brown tobacco. "Your favorite."

All four girls remained silent while Vester pulled a coin from his overall vest pocket and exchanged it for the tobacco. Then he reached into his front pocket and produced a jackknife, grinning at Hildy and Ruby.

Hildy flinched, remembering the time Vester had kidnapped them and they had used the same knife to cut their bonds and escape.

There was a strained silence while the moonshiner cut off a corner of the tobacco and transferred it to his mouth with the knife blade. He shifted the wad to his right cheek and spoke through yellow teeth. "Y'all purdy near ready to start back to school?" he asked, glancing at Hildy and Ruby, ignoring Bertha and Iris.

Hildy didn't want to talk to this man who was making her life miserable, but Ruby spoke up. "We ain't a-gonna go to school here," she announced, giving her blonde hair a shake. "We start a new one in Californy soon's we get home."

Vester closed the knife and slid it back into his pocket before answering. "Way I heard it," he said softly, looking at Hildy and Ruby and grinning through his untidy beard, "ye two ain't never goin' to leave this place."

He walked out the door, making the bell tinkle. To Hildy, the bell seemed like a warning alarm.

CHAPTER
ELEVEN
—

TRAGEDIES OLD AND NEW

Before the sound of the bell had died away, the door burst open and a wide-eyed boy of about eight ran inside. "Mr. Galvin!" the boy cried, panting hard and pointing through the big plate-glass window, "There's a fire yonder!"

Everyone ran out of the store. Hildy saw the smoke rising in the distance. She knew from the black color that a building was burning out of sight in a hollow between two mountainous ridges.

The merchant grabbed a short rope connected to an old dinner bell. It had once been used to call farmers from the fields for dinner or emergencies in their log homes. Hildy clapped both hands over her ears as Mr. Galvin jerked hard on the rope. The bell clanged loudly, summoning the volunteer fire department.

Hildy heard Iris exclaim, "That's mighty close to Gramp's and my house!"

"Maybe it is!" Bertha cried. "Come on!" She started running down the street with Iris beside her.

"Let's go see, too!" Hildy suggested.

"Wait! Here comes muh daddy!" Ruby replied.

When Nate Konning joined the girls, he said in a worried voice, "That's about where I met with Brother Rufus Hurley a while ago!"

The trio started running down the rocky road, following Bertha and Iris toward the towering black column of smoke.

Hildy asked anxiously, "If it is their house, do you suppose her grandfather's all right?"

"Sure hope so!" Nate replied, starting to pull away from the girls with his long running stride. "But excitement's not good for a man with a bum heart!"

Hildy and Ruby joined other curious people to make way for the volunteer-manned fire engine as it clattered up behind them. The two bays pulling the red pumper quickly drew away from the scattering crowd.

Nate's long legs carried him quickly past the others. Ruby was slightly ahead of Hildy and out of sight around a curve in the road when a terrible scream ripped across the mountains.

Sounds like Iris! Hildy thought, sprinting past the curve to where she could see into the wooded area. Her heart skipped a beat as she saw Iris running flat out, screaming at the top of her lungs. Hildy knew then that the burning house was indeed where Iris had lived with her ailing grandfather.

Hildy caught up to the circle of spectators just as the roof fell in with a great shower of sparks. Iris' cries were almost continuous, although Hildy couldn't see the girl because of onlookers in the way.

An anguished prayer for the old preacher's safety sprang to Hildy's lips as she pushed through the crowd, following Ruby. Hildy's eyes smarted from the smoke as she broke through the front line of spectators.

Hildy had never seen Iris' grandfather before, but she now glimpsed a white-haired man sprawled on the ground with one of the volunteer firemen kneeling beside him. The other firemen manned the pumper.

Iris threw herself down beside the old man. "Gramps!" she sobbed.

Hildy closed her eyes to block out the sight, but Iris' mournful cries could not be cut off.

A moment later, Hildy felt a hand on hers. She opened her eyes. Ruby said softly, "I jist talked to muh daddy. The preacher's dead. Daddy says he reckons it was his heart—the excitement an' all, 'cause he got out o' the house okay."

Hildy glanced toward the tragic scene before her. A blanket had been placed over the still form on the ground. Iris knelt beside him, rocking on her knees with low moaning sounds. Nate Konning tried to console her as Bertha stood silently behind them. Then Bertha slowly turned and walked away.

"Oh, Ruby!" Hildy said quietly. "Jist a little while ago, he was alive, helping Uncle Nate make plans for opening the church on Sunday. Now he's gone, and Iris is all alone in the world."

Ruby took her cousin's arm. "Come on. Ain't nothin' more we kin do right now."

"I've got to ask Uncle Nate or Iris if there's anything I can do."

Hildy approached the girl with Ruby at her side, but Iris didn't seem to hear when Hildy touched her and spoke. Uncle Nate looked up and motioned for Hildy and Ruby to go; he'd stay on for a while.

As the cousins walked slowly away, Hildy realized the fire was nearly out, but sparks still floated through the air. She cast anxious eyes at the surrounding forest.

"I guess the firemen'll keep the sparks from reaching the woods."

"Reckon so," Ruby agreed. "If'n it got away into them hills, dry as they be, it'd burn clean down to Little Rock afore anyone could stop it."

The girls returned to the general store to wait for Nate. The cousins told Mr. Galvin what they'd seen and explained about the old preacher's inviting Nate to preach on Sunday.

"Mr. Galvin, what'll happen to Iris?" Hildy asked.

Ruby snapped, "Who keers? She's meaner'n a snake at sheddin' time, so why should anyone keer about her?"

"You don't mean that, Ruby!" Hildy protested. "Sure, she's not been very nice to us, but her grandfather was the last living relative she had. Now she's all alone in the world!"

Ruby squirmed a little because Hildy's words struck close to home.

"Don't be too quick to judge Iris," The merchant cautioned. "Ruby, you have some idea of what it's like not having parents, because your mother's dead, and you didn't know until recently that your father was alive. Iris has had a rough life too."

Hildy said, "I've heard stories, Mr. Galvin, but I never knew for sure why Iris lived with her grandfather."

Ruby added, "Iris told us kids that her folks died in a street-car accident in Chicago a long time ago."

The merchant picked up a feather duster and absently passed it over the shelves. "That's only part of the story. Her grandfather told me what really happened. It probably made Iris the kind of person she is."

"What really happened?" Hildy asked.

Mr. Galvin sighed. "Iris' mother was always a little wild, I guess. She married Iris' father when she was barely sixteen. That was in Chicago where they were living at the time, and where Iris was born. Then, the way her grandfather told it, when Iris was about a year old, one day her parents were board-ing the streetcar, the wife holding Iris. All of a sudden she handed the baby to her husband who was already inside the streetcar. 'Here,' she said, 'you take her. I'm not cut out for being a mother.' "

Hildy was aghast. "You don't mean it!"

The merchant nodded. "Iris' father was so surprised he took the baby without thinking. Iris' mother turned away as the streetcar began to move. She tried to run across the street to get away, but a car coming the other way hit her, and she was killed."

"How awful!" Hildy exclaimed.

"Just ten days later to the day," Mr. Galvin continued, "Iris' father was hit by an ice truck. He lived a week."

Hildy closed her eyes and swallowed hard.

The merchant went on, "So Iris' grandfather—her only surviving relative—went to Chicago and made arrangements to be her guardian. He brought her back here and told Iris the truth when she was old enough to understand. But I guess it hurt too much to tell folks around here the whole truth, so Iris just told it the way she wanted to."

Hildy nodded, remembering the terrible feeling she'd had when Granny's lies had caused Molly to abandon her last summer.

Hildy walked over to Ruby, who was silently looking out the plate-glass window. The smoke had turned light gray and was drifting away. "No wonder Iris has such a nasty disposition," Hildy observed. "Having a mother who didn't want you is enough to make anyone mad at the world." She turned to look at the merchant. "What'll happen to her now?"

Mr. Galvin shook his head. "I don't know. Of course, Iris will have a place to stay for a while, because folks hereabouts have kind hearts. Maybe Bertha's family will take her in, although I don't see how they can feed another mouth. But after that—who knows?"

Hildy suddenly felt sorry for the girl who had helped make her life difficult in Possum Hollow. But she identified with Iris for a different reason. Hildy had already imagined what it would be like to lose her grandmother in death. Now Iris faced not only the reality of her grandfather's death, but the awful emptiness of having no family left at all.

Hildy felt blessed because she had a family. "Ruby," she announced, "I'm going for a walk."

"Whereabouts?"

"I don't know. Just walking. I need to think." She started for the door, then stopped. "I'll go back to Granny's later. What're you and Uncle Nate going to do?"

"Since muh grandmother done kicked us out, reckon we'll stay at Seth and Rachel's place."

"I want to see them too. After I think a while, I'll probably see you there."

It never occurred to either Hildy or Ruby that their unexpected arrival at Seth and Rachel's would be anything but welcome. Because company was rare, most mountain folk appreciated any visitors.

"Reckon muh daddy an' me'll be here a spell yet," Ruby said thoughtfully. "Since there's no other preacher man hereabouts, they may ask Daddy to hold the funeral service."

Hildy nodded, waved goodbye to Mr. Galvin, and walked out into the muggy air. She glanced hopefully at the sky, but there was no sign of a cloud. There would be no rain today.

Hildy's thoughts zigged and zagged like a summer lightning storm as she left the small town and turned into the forest. Dry twigs snapped under her feet.

Nearly ninety percent of the county was in woodland, steep and stony, with mixed strands of hardwoods, mostly oak and hickory with some shortleaf pine and eastern red cedar. Hildy pushed deeper into the woods, passing native woody plants like grapes, dogwood, and blackberries.

Hildy's mind wasn't really on the plants, although she was alert for wildlife. White-tailed deer and black bear had been hunted almost to extinction, but the girl thought she might see some wild turkeys. Instead, she saw only thrushes, woodpeckers, and a hawk on the wing.

Sure would hate to be in here if a fire started, she told herself, carefully skirting some berry vines.

Soon she approached her destination, one of her favorite "thinking places," as she called it. She glimpsed a sandstone escarpment ahead. It rose above the trees, somewhat resembling the flat top of Thunder Mountain in California. But the faces of these long, cliff-like ridges were carved into niches, unlike the sheer castle-like sides of the mountain back home.

Because she was alone, Hildy allowed herself to speak aloud. "California's my home. Someday, we'll have our 'forever home' there, too. But I can't leave Granny in danger of Vester. And he's not going to let Ruby or me leave—not if he can help it."

The girl's mind jumped. "Poor Iris! I feel so sorry for her. Wish there was something I could do."

Hildy eased across an open meadow and then back into

mixed stands of oak and shortleaf pine. She would have liked
to scale the precipitous escarpment and sit there where it would
be more inspiring to look over the endless ridges. Because that
was impractical now, Hildy found the shelter of a white oak and
sat down, spreading her dress across her knees.

All her problems and concerns flooded through her mind,
causing a dull ache. "What'll I do?" she asked herself. She raised
her eyes to the sheer sandstone battlements rising above her.

A verse came to mind. "I will lift up mine eyes unto the hills
from whence cometh my help."

"Lord," Hildy said softly, "I need that help. There are lots of
problems—" She let the prayer trail off while her mind quickly
reviewed the problems she'd recently shared with Ruby and
Uncle Nate. Now there was Iris too, for whom Hildy had never
thought she'd feel sorry.

Her thoughts jumped again. She asked herself, "What was
it Brother Ben once told me a person must do to succeed at
anything?"

The former Texas Ranger was a member of Hildy's church at
Lone River. He'd counseled, "Have a purpose, a plan, and then
persevere. Purpose! Plan! Persevere!" The words came back to
the girl, distinct as bells on a frosty morning.

Hildy sat up, savoring the wisdom of the words. "I know
what my purpose is," she thought. "But I need a plan. Then, I
need to stick to it until I achieve my purpose." She jumped up
and brushed off her dress. "I need a plan!"

It did not come in a blinding flash of revelation, but it came,
slowly at first, then faster and faster. It reminded her of when
a vinegar barrel was first opened and poured. It gave a sort of
glurg, almost stopped, then another *glurg*, faster this time; and
then another and another until the pungent liquid poured out
in a solid stream.

Hildy turned away from the escarpment, thoughts spilling
through her mind. By the time she topped the hill above Granny's log house, Hildy knew what she had to do as the first part
of her plan.

She opened the unlocked back door and entered Granny's

main room. Through the door into the lean-to kitchen, Hildy could see her grandmother mixing her daily cornbread batter with a wooden spoon.

"Granny," Hildy called. "I'm back."

Granny dropped the spoon and turned. "Glad yo're here! Muh poor ol' fingers is so stiff I cain't rightly close muh hands. The spoon keeps a-slippin' away."

For a second, Hildy felt sorry for her grandmother's arthritic condition. Then the girl remembered that a moment before Granny had had no trouble holding the spoon. Hildy suspected Granny was playing on her sympathy to help keep her here.

Hildy started the first step in her plan. "Granny, I overheard what you and Vester said today."

The sharp, dark eyes snapped with disapproval. "Ye mean ye was a-sneakin' around, spyin'?"

"I'm ashamed, but yes, I did. I know Vester went to California to bring me back here because he thinks you put a hex on him."

"He's so ignorant he don't know he's ignorant!"

"You've got to tell him there's no such thing as a hex, and that you didn't put one on him. Then he'll leave me alone, and he won't hurt you, either. As it is now, your life's in danger. Maybe Ruby's and mine too."

"Will ye stay here with me if'n I do?"

Hildy shook her head. "No, Granny. As soon as you do what I've already asked you, Ruby and I will head for home in California."

The hope went out of the old woman's eyes and her voice changed to a whine. "Ye don't love me!"

"I love you. You know that!" Hildy hurried around the table and threw her arms around Granny.

"It ain't no good to get old all by yoreself," Granny said sadly.

For a moment, Hildy's heart twisted in sympathy, then she remembered her plan. "Granny, if you and your sister make up, you could live together and take care of each other while Ruby and I are back in California."

"Don't mention that woman's name in muh house!"

"Then come back to California with me."

"I ain't never gonna leave these hills!"

"Granny, please—!"

"I don't want to hear another word about it!"

Slowly, Hildy took a deep breath. "I thought I'd figured this out right for everybody. Guess I was wrong." She turned toward the door.

"Where ye goin'?" Granny asked.

"I'm going to stay with some friends tonight. The Hightons live near here."

Hildy almost ran from the house, hurt by the failure of her first two ideas, and knowing that time was running out.

CHAPTER
TWELVE

WHEN OLD FRIENDS MEET

Hildy picked up her long dress and ran hard from Granny's log house to the top of the nearest ridge. *Sure hope I don't miss Ruby and Uncle Nate*, she thought as she crested the wooded mountain and looked down the other side.

On the unpaved and rocky road below, she saw a bay mare clattering along on iron-shod hooves. Hildy stopped running and shaded her eyes against the sun's glare to see who was in the buggy. She hoped it was her cousin and uncle in a rented rig, but Hildy instantly knew that wasn't possible. The horse was headed toward town, not away from it.

Hildy started running again, thinking that she could look at the roadway to see if another buggy had recently passed. She would be able to tell by the horse's hoofprints which way it was going. *Maybe Uncle Nate and Ruby have already gone on toward Seth and Rachel's place*, she told herself.

Hildy reached the road, puffing hard, just as the town-bound rig started around a slight curve. Hildy glimpsed a man and woman inside the buggy.

Hildy blinked in surprise, took another look and let out a happy yell, "Seth! Rachel!"

The man leaned out of the buggy and looked back from the left side of the light, single-seated, four-wheeled carriage. His square jaw jutted defiantly from a powerful neck. "Whoa!" he called, pulling back on the reins. "Rachel, honey, look yonder!"

Hildy started running toward the bu ˑ ʞy as a pretty woman stuck her head out on the buggy's right side. "Hildy!" she called, waving.

The man wrapped the lines around the buggy-whip socket and jumped down. He helped his tall, slender wife to the ground as Hildy dashed up, breathless but delighted.

"Seth! Rachel!" Hildy cried. "It's so good to see you! Ruby and her father were headed for your place, and I was trying to—"

"Ruby's *father*?" the young woman interjected, her gray eyes wide in surprise. Giving Hildy a quick, warm hug, she stepped back and looked her in the face. "Did you say her father?"

"Yes! We found him!" She turned to Seth who extended his right hand in greeting, but changed his mind and gave Hildy a strong bear hug instead. "Oh Seth, there's so much to talk about!" Hildy exclaimed.

"What on earth brings ye back to these parts, Hildy?" he asked, releasing her.

"Oh, so many things! I'll need some time to explain it all to you," Hildy answered.

The tall, lanky young man took Hildy and Rachel by their elbows and steered them toward the buggy. "Reckon we can talk an' ride at the same time," he said, smiling.

Hildy's mind flooded with memories as she sat down between her two friends. Seth retrieved the reins and called to his horse, "Giddyup, Bess!"

Above the clip-clopping sound of the horse's shoes, Rachel asked, "Now tell us what you and Ruby are doing back in the Ozarks. And what about her father?" Before Hildy could respond, she added, "And whatever happened to that terrible man who was chasing you girls? What was his name—Vester?"

"Yes. Vester. But I don't know where to start!"

"Then jist jump in somewheres," Seth suggested.

Hildy nodded, briefly recalling her and Ruby's meeting with Seth and Rachel last June, and how they had taken the girls in Seth's Model T Ford to Hildy's paternal grandparents in Illinois, with Vester following close behind.

"Then," Hildy concluded, "after you two went on to Chicago, Vester caught Ruby and me alone in town and held us prisoner in an old cattle car. He was planning to take us back to the Ozarks, but we escaped, found my family again, and we all went on to California."

"Oh, how awful!" Rachel exclaimed, "I'm so glad you were able to escape!" Then she added pensively, "When Ruby found her father, she wanted to bring him back to the Ozarks. Right?"

Hildy nodded, explaining how they'd found Nate, and then Vester's determination to keep the girls here. She was just finishing her story when another horse and buggy approached them.

"It's Ruby and Uncle Nate!" she exclaimed. "They're heading for your place."

Both buggies came to a halt, and Ruby was warmly welcomed by the Hightons. Then she proudly introduced her long-lost father.

After the breathless exchange of news, Hildy asked Seth and Rachel, "Where were you two headed, anyway?"

"Possum Hollow." Seth pointed in the general direction. "We need some store-bought things we can't grow or make ourselves. Say, why don't y'all come into town with us and then stay the night at our house?"

Everyone eagerly agreed, and Hildy took her seat again between Seth and Rachel. Nate turned his buggy around and followed. Before they reached town, Hildy had told them of the fire and the death of Iris' grandfather.

At Mr. Galvin's general store, there was more talk about Rufus Hurley's death and upcoming funeral. Nate had agreed to conduct the services in the tiny church the old pastor had served for so long.

Shadows started to fill the valley when the two rigs headed out of town. This time, Ruby rode with the Hightons, and Uncle Nate let Hildy drive his rented horse. After they were on their way, he said, "Ruby tol' me ye went to think today."

Realizing that was her uncle's way of getting her to talk about it, Hildy filled him in on everything from her quiet time of praying and planning, to the utter failure of her first two suggestions with Granny.

Nate observed thoughtfully, "Those two women sure are set in their ways, but don't ye give up, Hildy!"

"I won't. At first I felt really bad, but now I'm going to try something else."

Before she could explain her plan, the buggy topped a rise, and Hildy was looking down on the Highton's log house. Again, memories flooded her mind. She reminisced to Nate about the first time she'd seen the place.

"But they've built on to it since then," Hildy finished, looking over the house. She swung the buggy into the yard beside the Highton's mare.

Seth had already stepped down and helped Ruby and Rachel to the ground. "Seth, I see you've added lean-tos at the side and back of the house," Hildy said.

"Yes," Seth explained, "Rachel didn't like the place lookin' like a bachelor lived here, so we added a kitchen in back and an extra room for the baby."

"Seth!" Rachel, obviously embarrassed, elbowed her husband in the ribs.

"A baby?" Hildy exclaimed, looking at the couple warmly.

"Someday," Rachel replied.

Seth cleared his throat and changed the subject, "Hildy, do ye remember my old Model T?" He pointed toward a harness shed where the post-war Ford rested.

"Do I? That was the first car Ruby and I ever saw!"

"Don't run much no more," Seth explained. "But the mare pulls this buggy anywhere Rachel an' me want to go."

He turned to his wife. "Honey, why don't ye take the gals

inside? Nate'n me'll put the horses away an' be in directly with the things from town."

Hildy took in the layout of the Highton home—a screened-in back porch, a combination parlor, a bedroom in the loft, plus the new lean-to kitchen and nursery.

"Make yourselves at home while I fix us something cold to drink," Rachel said to the girls.

"I'd rather talk to you," Hildy said, following the woman into the kitchen, "if you don't mind."

"I'd love that," Rachel said with a smile.

"Me, too," Ruby added. "Tell us about the baby."

They were still talking when Seth entered the kitchen with a twenty-five-pound lard bucket, and a fifty-pound sack of flour under his arm. Nate carried a five-gallon can of kerosene with a potato stuck on the spout for a stopper, and a sack of dry red beans.

Hildy heard Seth say to Nate, "Like I said, I wasn't what y'all could call a church-goin' man till me'n Rachel got hitched. But we been goin' reg'lar lately, so we'll sure miss Brother Rufus. But I'd be mighty proud to drive around an' tell folks yo're a-gonna preach come Sunday. Might help ye have a better turn-out."

"Much obliged, Seth."

Hildy followed the men back into the parlor. "Uncle Nate, what about the funeral?"

"It'll be tomorrow. Some of the menfolks are a-diggin' the grave now. Others'll be layin' the brother out tonight at one of the homes. After supper Seth and me'll go back into town to be sure the church's ready, and then stop by where Iris is stayin' and see if we can be of some comfort to the poor girl."

Hildy had attended only a few country funerals. In summer, the burial was prompt, no later than the next day. Since there were no funeral homes, friends dressed the body and placed it in a handmade wooden coffin at the home of the deceased. In the pastor's case, because his home had burned, a neighbor had offered his house. Neighbors would come to sit and mourn with the lone survivor—Iris.

"I'd like to ride along, if I can, please," Hildy said.

"Tonight?" her uncle asked. "Are you sure?"

"Yes. Since everyone from miles around usually comes to sit with the family, maybe Ruby's grandmother will be there. I'd like to talk to her about a couple of things."

Ruby stuck her head into the parlor. "Ye plumb lost yore mind, Hildy? What'd ye want to see her for?"

"Oh, it's part of a plan I've got."

"What plan?" Ruby demanded. She came into the parlor, wiping her hands on a flour sack that was used for a towel.

"Well, for one thing, I'd like to ask her to make up with my grandmother."

Ruby snorted. "Ain't no way she's a-gonna do that!"

"I have to ask, at least," Hildy said with quiet conviction. "You want to come along?"

"Yo're forgettin' she done kicked me'n muh daddy outta her house! Well, muh daddy, anyway, an' it's the same's doin' it to me!"

"No, I'm not forgetting. But death has a way of making people think. Sometimes they soften a little, maybe even change."

"Not her!" Ruby said emphatically. "No more'n yore ol' granny'd change! I don't see no sense a-goin'!"

Hildy added, "I also want to talk to Iris."

"Iris?" Ruby's asked in disbelief. "She hates the ground ye walk on!"

"Maybe. Anyway, I want her to know I'm sorry about her grandfather's death. C'mon, Ruby, go along with me."

She shook her head. "I'm sorry the ol' preacher man died, but I cain't feel sorry for Iris, not after what she 'n' Big Bertha done to you 'n' me when we went to school here!"

"You don't really mean that, Ruby!" Hildy protested.

Ruby shook her head again. "I'm a-gonna stay with Rachel."

Rachel came from the kitchen, carrying a potato she'd been peeling. She glanced at Hildy, sensing the girl's deep emotional struggle. "If we take both buggies," Rachel suggested, "we can all go tonight."

Hildy flashed a grateful smile at Rachel, but Ruby's voice

snapped, "Vester'll more'n likely be a-hangin' around in the dark somewheres, watchin' us!"

"He won't try anything while Uncle Nate and Seth are around!" Hildy protested.

Ruby shivered and made a face. "Ugh! Jist the way he looks at me makes muh skin crawl!"

"Me, too," Hildy admitted. "But I think Granny's in more danger than we are, that is, as long as we don't try leaving here."

Ruby rubbed her bare arms. "Lookee thar! Gooseflesh big as hen's eggs, jist a-thinkin' 'bout Vester!"

Hildy thought of another way to persuade her cousin to ride into town with her. "We both have reason to be afraid of Vester, Ruby, but are you sure your *real* reason for not going isn't because you're afraid to be near the graveyard at night?"

Ruby unsuspectingly took the bait. "I ain't skeered—jist 'cause some folks *say* they's haints thar!"

Hildy had to fight the triumphant smile that threatened to sneak across her face. "Then you'll come tonight?"

Too late, Ruby's face revealed she'd been trapped. She gulped a couple of times, then shrugged. "Reckon I kin come along and protect ye, Hildy."

After supper, Hildy rode between Seth and Rachel in the first buggy, and Ruby and her father followed in the rented rig. Because the moon hadn't risen, the night was black, darkness filling the wooded hills and valleys. Hildy found the ride creepy and strange. In California there were few horses and buggies; she was used to cars with headlights at night.

Because Seth's old Model T wasn't running, he had provided both buggies with kerosene lanterns. The weak lights rested on the floorboards. If Nate or Seth heard another horse approaching in the darkness, they would lift the lantern to warn the other driver. Neither of the horses needed the lights, because they could see much better at night than people.

Conversation lagged, and then Rachel cleared her throat. "Hildy, you said that you wanted to talk to Ruby's grandmother about a couple of things. I understand you're trying to get her to make up with your grandmother, but do you mind my asking what else you want to talk to Mrs. Skaggs about?"

Hildy started to answer, then the impossibility of what she had in mind struck hard.

She gripped Rachel's hand in the darkness and whispered, "It's part of a plan that came to me while I was thinking out in the woods today. But suddenly, I'm afraid it'll fail just like the ideas I tried on Granny! Oh, Rachel, what if I fail again?"

CHAPTER THIRTEEN

A FRIGHTENING NIGHT CHASE

Hildy felt sad as they passed the little church on the way to a neighbor's house where visitors would come to pay their respects to Iris and the memory of her grandfather. The moon had just risen, showing the crosses and headstones in the cemetery.

Seth stopped the horse in front of the house, which was tucked back in among the trees. Hildy saw that other buggies and wagons were already there. Small clumps of people stood near the teams, talking in low voices.

Hildy stepped down from Seth's buggy as Ruby hurried over from her father's rig. She gripped Hildy's bare arm and whispered, "Didja see it when we passed the graveyard?"

"See what?"

"The light! A strange light, movin' through the headstones!"

"It was probably just one of the gravediggers carrying a lantern to find his way home."

"No! It was a haint!" Ruby said hoarsely.

Hildy felt her cousin's hand tremble on her arm. Hildy placed her hand on Ruby's. "There's no such thing! Quit scaring your-self. Now, come on, let's go in."

Ruby held back. "I don't like bein' around dead people."

"We've got to pay our respects, and maybe be a help to Iris."

With Ruby trailing reluctantly, Hildy followed her Uncle Nate, Rachel, and Seth across the yard toward two lighted lan-terns that had been placed on the porch rails to guide visitors to the front door.

The adults nodded somberly to the small clumps of people standing in the darkness. As the five new arrivals mounted the wooden stairs, Hildy automatically rose up on her tiptoes in an effort to walk more quietly. She noticed others did the same. It made her wonder why people always seemed to be quiet in the presence of the dead.

Hildy felt Ruby's hand gripping the back of her elbow. "I jist cain't go in thar!" she whispered.

Hildy lowered her voice. "Yes, you can. Just stay close to me."

"I'd rather stay out here."

"No you wouldn't," Hildy whispered. "Vester could be out there in the darkness someplace. Better come inside with us."

Two lamps on wall brackets cast a pale, silvery half-circle of light about the middle-aged woman who attended the door. Hildy didn't recognize her.

The woman did not speak, but stepped aside signifying an invitation to enter. In the dim lamplight Hildy noticed an old organ in one corner and heavy furniture lining the walls. The room smelled musty, as if it had been closed up. Hildy could hear someone weeping softly.

Peering through the faint light of the two bracket-lamps, Hildy could see Iris sitting in a big chair, her legs drawn up under her body. She faced the wall, but Hildy could detect tear streaks on her left cheek.

Hildy wanted to reach out to her with some sort of comfort, but the woman who had let them in motioned for them to follow her through a large sliding door. They entered a room lit by a single reflector lamp on the opposite wall. The pale yellow rays fell on a plain wooden coffin that rested on two sawhorses in the middle of the room. Some mourners stood silently gazing at the form in the casket, while others sat nearby. No one spoke a word.

Ruby clutched Hildy's hand from behind. She whispered hoarsely, "Don't make me walk by thar!"

Hildy nodded and whispered to Rachel ahead of her. "I'm going back into the other room with Ruby."

The two girls returned to where Iris still huddled in a corner. There was no one else in the room. Hildy walked over to her but didn't know what to say. She reached out and lightly touched the girl's shoulder.

Slowly, Iris turned and looked up. "I just can't believe he's gone," she said brokenly.

All the mean things Iris and Bertha had done when Hildy lived in Possum Hollow flooded into her mind. Iris had talked and acted so tough then. Now she was crushed and broken, weeping alone.

Hildy managed to say softly, "I'm sorry."

Iris sniffed and dabbed at her eyes with a white handkerchief. "You two are the only kids that've come."

Hildy was surprised. "Where's Bertha?"

Iris shrugged and spoke bitterly, "Guess she couldn't stand coming. Maybe she's afraid, or maybe she feels bad too, but it can't be as bad I feel! Gramps is gone!" Iris sobbed, gripping Hildy's and Ruby's hands. "Oh, what'm I a-gonna do now?"

"Let's all go outside," Hildy suggested.

Iris seemed anxious for the change, but tensed as the girls stepped out. The people standing around under the trees stared at them.

"This way," Iris said softly, leading Hildy and Ruby around the side of the house to the back yard.

The girls stopped near the well curbing where the moon shown brightly. Hildy could see that Iris' eyes were still puffy from crying.

Not knowing where to begin, Hildy took a deep breath and blurted, "Is there anything we can do?"

Iris shook her head. "Gramps was the only person in the world left of my family. Now he's—" She broke off with a sob.

Hildy swallowed a lump in her own throat. "Where—where're you going to live now?"

"I don't know." Iris' voice was flat, dull, without feeling. "He was all I had." She glanced toward the house where her grandfather lay. "Even though he'd been havin' bad spells with his heart, I didn't think he'd really—die."

Ruby hadn't said a word, and Hildy could tell at a glance that her cousin was unmoved. Ruby obviously didn't like Iris, and Hildy couldn't blame her for that, but in spite of everything, Hildy was touched by Iris' situation.

"Could you stay with Bertha?"

"Her folks already have a bunch of kids. They won't want another mouth to feed."

"Do you know anyone else who might have room for you?"

Iris slowly shook her head. "I guess me 'n' Bertha've made just about everybody mad at us one time or another. Most folks would just as soon run us off like stray cats for all the things we done to their kids."

Hildy was shocked to hear Ruby whisper under her breath, "Serves ye right, too!"

Hildy shot a warning look at her cousin, but Iris didn't seem to hear the remark.

The moonlight glistened on Iris' damp face. "Hildy, Ruby, I just wanna say I'm sorry for all the things me 'n' Bertha did to you two."

"It's okay," Hildy said without hesitation, reaching out to pat Iris' shoulder. "Forget it."

"But I can't! It's even harder now that you two have come to see me when not another kid from school did. Not Bertha, not Elston—"

"They'll probably come later," Hildy said.

Iris shrugged. "Anyway, I'd be obliged if you'd both let me try to make it up to you."

Hildy saw an opening to pursue her second reason for coming. It was part of the plan she'd made below the sandstone escarpment. "You got along fine with your grandfather?"

Iris sniffed and nodded. "Always did. Fact is, I get along just fine with all old folks. Maybe that's 'cause I grew up with Gramps, and most o' his friends was old. Well, 'course, there was others who came to church where he preached, but mostly it was old folks who came to visit us."

"Do you know Ruby's grandmother?" Hildy asked.

"Mrs. Skaggs? Yeah. Why?"

"Do you get along with her?"

"Better'n most folks, I reckon."

"How about my grandmother?"

"Same, I guess. I don't see either one too often, but we always got along tolerable well. Why're you asking?"

"Yeah!" Ruby exclaimed in a tone that sounded more like Iris. "Why're you asking?"

Hildy ignored Ruby and asked Iris, "Have you seen Ruby's grandmother here tonight? She lives close by."

"No sign of her yet."

Ruby tugged on Hildy's elbow. "Why'd you ask?"

"I wanted to talk to her about something before I said anything to you or Iris, but, as long as I've got the chance—" Hildy paused, then finished in a rush. "Iris, in a few days Ruby and I are going back to California with my Uncle Nate—Ruby's father. My family needs me because my father may have to go off looking for work again, and my stepmother'll need help with the kids. When Ruby and I are gone, that'll leave both our grandmothers alone. They're getting along in years, and they need somebody around. You need someone too, Iris, a place to live, and someone to care for you. What do you think? Could you live with one or both of our grandmothers?"

Ruby sputtered in surprise, "Muh grandma couldn't get along with me, her only blood kin! What makes ye think she'd cotton to Iris? And yore granny—she lied to Molly and done ye wrong! Why, the devil hisself couldn't get along with them two! Iris don't stand a chance neither."

Iris' expression was sad and weary in the moonlight. "Ruby's right. Is that all you wanted to talk to me about, Hildy?"

"Yes," Hildy admitted. "Only I wanted to talk to Ruby's grandmother first, but since she's not here, and you are—"

"I'm obliged to ye," Iris said honestly. "But there's no way in this world it'd work out. Everybody around here knows how mean-tempered those women can be. No offense to either of you two."

Iris rose suddenly and hurried into the house through the back door.

"That shore was a dumb idee!" Ruby growled.

Hildy didn't reply. She felt such a sick, sad feeling inside at the failure of still another effort to provide for her grandmother and her sister. In silence, she walked around the outside of the house to the front yard. Ruby followed, still grumbling about Hildy's idea.

The front yard was deserted. Hildy heard a team of horses and a wagon pulling away, and in the soft moonlight she could see two horses and buggies already moving down the quiet road. At the same time, another buggy pulled up and stopped.

The cousins stood silently in the deep shadows, waiting to see who had arrived. They heard a man's voice ask, "Shall I wait, Mrs. Skaggs?"

"Of course!" her voice cracked with annoyance. "I'll only be a few minutes."

Hildy whispered, "It's your grandmother."

"Yeah," Ruby whispered back. "Reckon I'd best stay out o' her sight, seein' as how she throwed me'n muh daddy out o' her house!"

Hildy sucked in her breath. "He's inside! Maybe I can slip in and warn—"

"Too late!" Ruby interrupted. "She's already a-walkin' up the steps! Ye cain't get ahead of her now!"

"Maybe I can stop her outside! Run around to the back door and tell your daddy. He's got to get to the church anyway."

Without waiting to see what Ruby did, Hildy called softly, "Grandma Skaggs, it's me—Hildy Corrigan."

The old woman stopped at the foot of the wooden stairs and turned around to peer into the darkness. "Where's Ruby?"

"Around," Hildy replied vaguely, hurrying up to the porch. "May I talk to you a moment?"

"What about?" The old woman's voice was tinged with suspicion.

"I guess you know about Iris' grandfather—"

"Course I know!" Mrs. Skaggs broke in. "Why'd ye reckon I'm out here this time o' night? I come to pay muh respects, like any decent Christian would!"

Hildy tried not to let the biting tone get to her. She wondered why almost everyone she knew had loving, caring grandparents, while she and Ruby had two sharp-tongued, bitter sisters for grandmothers.

"Mrs. Skaggs, I was talking to Iris a few minutes ago. She's got no living relative in the world now, and nobody around here to take her in and give her a place to live."

"Let her live alone! I do. So does that cantankerous sister o' mine! In fact, lots o' folks live alone."

Hildy felt her hopes start to slip. "But Iris is young and needs somebody who's older and wiser to live with, someone who'll give her more than just a place to eat and sleep."

"Hildy, if'n yo're a-tryin' to get me to take that gal in, forget it! I know all about her and Bertha. Couple o' the o'neriest kids in these here mountains!"

Something snapped in Hildy. Sudden anger surged through her and she blurted, "Ornery?" The word exploded into the night. Then she repeated a phrase she'd often heard her late mother say, "You ever hear of the pot calling the kettle black?"

"Ye a-callin' me o'nery, Hildy Corrigan?"

There was a sharp challenge to the old woman's voice, but Hildy's rare temper was aroused. Her stubborn streak erupted into full force. "Excuse me for saying it, but you and my grandmother are about the—"

Hildy snapped her mouth shut so hard her teeth clicked, cutting off the angry words. "I'm sorry," she finished.

She whirled and stumbled away into the night, the anger still bitter on her tongue and guilt slicing her conscience into painful ribbons. She vaguely heard Ruby's grandmother ascend the wooden stairs. She was also aware that Ruby was running toward her from the back of the house, softly calling her name. But Hildy didn't stop.

"Oh, why?" she moaned through clenched teeth, gazing up at the star-sprinkled heavens. "Why does everything I try turn sour?"

She was almost to the cemetery, the church just beyond, when Hildy stopped, panting hard, her lungs aching. She slowed and waited for Ruby to catch up.

"Where ye headin'?" Ruby asked.

"To the church. To wait for Uncle Nate."

Ruby glanced anxiously at the moon-drenched cemetery. "Why don't we wait an' ride in the buggy with him?"

Before Hildy could answer, a hound bayed somewhere behind them. Both girls whirled, looking up toward the source of the sound. Against the pale moon, riding along the base of the wooded mountain, a heavy-set man in a slouch hat followed the hound, coming straight toward the girls.

"Get 'em, Scratch!" the man's voice urged the dog.

"That's Vester!" Hildy whispered.

"Let's run!" Ruby turned toward the way they'd come.

Hildy grabbed her arm. "Not that way! He'll cut us off! This way!"

"Through the graveyard?"

"It's the only way!" Hildy exclaimed. "Come on!"

"I cain't do it!"

"Would you rather stay here and wait for Vester?"

"Course not! But don't run off 'n' leave me with all them dead people!"

Grabbing Ruby's hand, Hildy pushed through the small wooden gate and broke into a run past the first tombstones. A vine caught her other arm and she jerked away, as Ruby sobbed in fear as they fled through the moonlit cemetery toward the only other gate.

Behind them, the hound bayed eagerly, closing in fast on his quarry.

Hildy stole a glance backward. "Where'd Vester go?" she asked in alarm.

Ruby looked back too. "Maybe that weren't Vester a-tall! Maybe it's a haint!"

Chapter Fourteen

A STARTLING ANNOUNCEMENT

There's no such thing!" Hildy puffed, dodging around a bush that partially grew into the cemetery path.

Ruby obviously wasn't convinced. Hildy heard her cousin fight to control frightened sobs as the girls continued on the eerie path through the cemetery.

Hildy held so tightly to Ruby's hand that she was almost towed through the maze of tombstones, shrubs, and trees. The baying hound, gaining behind them, urged them on.

In a clear section of the path, Hildy glanced back again. "I still don't see Vester!" she exclaimed.

"That's 'cause it was a haint!"

"No! It was Vester's voice! But where'd he go?"

"They's only one way out o' this graveyard now, and that's the gate by the church. Maybe they's somebody thar, an' we'll be safe!"

Hildy could barely see the front gate. "If Vester gets too close," she panted, "we'll scream! That'll bring somebody to help us!"

Ruby puffed, "Ain't nobody kin he'p if a haint gets ye!"

"I told you, there's no such thing!" Hildy repeated, ducking low to avoid an overhanging branch. "It's just your imagin—!"

Her words caught in her throat as she raised her head again, and slid to a halt before a marble tombstone with a winged angel on top.

Ruby almost collided with Hildy, then sucked in her breath sharply. "What's the matter?" she whispered.

"Shhh! I saw something move up ahead by the gate!"

"It's the haint!" Ruby whispered hoarsely.

"I said, 'Shhh!' "

For a long moment, Hildy held her breath and peered anxiously toward their only way out of the cemetery.

"I don't see nothin'!" Ruby whispered.

"I don't see it now, but something moved up there!" Hildy squatted down, pulling Ruby beside her. "Let's hide and watch for a minute until we see what it was."

"Ye crazy?" Ruby cried in a hoarse whisper. "Let's get outta here!"

"No, wait! Maybe Vester circled around and got to the front gate of ahead of us." Hildy strained to see through the pale moonlight. "Maybe he left his dog behind to keep us from turning back, so we'd run into him."

Suddenly, something moved again at the front gate. Hildy gasped at the sight of a white object that fluttered like a sheet on her stepmother's clothesline.

Ruby let out a tiny, frightened squeak. "See? I told ye it was a haint!"

Hildy ignored her racing heart and almost stopped breathing as she tried to identify the strange object floating ahead of them. Vester's hound still bayed in the background.

Then her mind warned, *You can't stay here and you can't go back. You've got to go ahead!* But her feet wouldn't move; they seemed frozen to the ground.

The hair on the back of Hildy's neck stood on end as a low moaning sound billowed out from the image before them.

"Oooohhhhh!"

Ruby jumped to her feet, yanking Hildy's arm so hard they both stumbled and almost fell. "It moaned! It's a-comin' for us, Hildy!"

Hildy regained her balance. "I think it's Vester!" she whispered loudly.

The hound bellowed deeply, "Bahooh!"

Hildy spun around just in time to see the dog crash against the closed wooden gate so hard it was almost torn from its hinges.

"He's a-comin' through the fence!" Ruby screeched. "We're trapped!"

Hildy looked again at the strange white object. It moved again, making Ruby clutch Hildy's hand even harder.

"I tell you, it's a-comin' for us!" Ruby cried.

Hildy's mouth was dry from fear, but she managed to breathe, "Somebody's coming!" Lifting her head from behind the bush where the girls crouched, she added, "See? Beyond the gate. With a lantern!"

"No! It's another haint!" Ruby wailed.

"It's a man!" Hildy jumped up and yelled. "Hey!"

The lantern stopped swinging. Hildy waved and raised her voice, "We're over here!"

"Who's there?" the man called, lifting the lantern high. "Who's calling?"

Hildy exclaimed, "It's Mr. Galvin! Come on!"

"No!" Ruby's voice was high and thin with fright. "It's another haint a-tryin' to fool us!"

"No, it's not." Hildy cupped her hands to call. "Is that you, Mr. Galvin?"

"Yes!" the answer came. "Who's out there?"

"It's Hildy—and Ruby! Wait for us!"

Hildy freed herself from her cousin's frantic grip, but Ruby shrieked again. "I ain't a-goin' past that haint at the gate!"

The hound bayed close behind, his toenails making a scratching sound as he scrambled to climb over a tombstone.

"We can't let that dog get us!" Hildy snapped. "He'll probably tear us to pieces!" She grabbed Ruby's hand and raced for the gate. "We're coming, Mr. Galvin!"

Ruby held back, trying to dig her heels into the dirt as Hildy sprinted toward the white object that blocked their way to the gate. "Yo're gonna run right over that haint!" she whimpered. "Or go right through it!"

Suddenly the apparition sprang up, tall as a man. It's bat-like wings flashed wide. Hildy slid to a stop, her throat paralyzed with fear. Ruby bumped into her so hard both girls tripped over a tombstone and tumbled head first into a bush.

Desperately, Hildy struggled to her feet, almost falling again. The mysterious white object was fleeing along the outside of the fence, away from the gate, toward the wooded mountain.

"Lookee!" Ruby whispered in awe. "We done skeered the haint!"

Hildy started to answer but hesitated when the ghostly figure stopped in the shadow of a tree. Then they heard a tooting sound. The hound, just yards behind the girls, slid to a halt.

"That's a hunter's horn," Hildy whispered. She'd heard cow's horns before, used to recall hounds from the trail of a raccoon. "A man's blowing it. It must be Vester!"

"Ye mean he run ahead of us and hid to skeer us?"

Hildy nodded. "And now he's calling in his dog. Come on!" Hildy urged her cousin, trotting toward Mr. Galvin beyond the cemetery gate.

The merchant held the lantern high as the girls ran up. "Who was that running into the woods?" he asked. "Looked kind of spooky!"

"A man in a sheet," Hildy replied grimly. "Vester was trying to scare us!"

"Oh, and what were you girls doing out here in the grave-yard?" Mr. Galvin asked.

Hildy almost laughed with relief. She put her arm around Ruby's shoulder. "We'll tell you on the way to the church," she said.

The girls had almost finished retelling their adventure when they reached the front door of the sanctuary. "It's kind of strange for a grown man to scare a couple of girls like that," Mr. Galvin said, "but everybody knows Vester's a little strange. You girls best be careful of him."

Hildy nodded, thinking Vester was playing a game of cat and mouse with them. She thought too, that he could be just as deadly as a cat with a couple of helpless mice. But Hildy didn't say anything because they arrived just ahead of Ruby's father, Seth, and Rachel. By lamplight, everything was checked and found ready for tomorrow's funeral service.

The cousins had decided they would tell the others about their experience on the buggy ride back to the Highton place. Hildy also told Seth and Rachel about her conversations with Iris and Ruby's grandmother. She imagined that Ruby was also repeating these conversations in her father's rented buggy where she rode.

When they finally all reached the Highton home, the situation was discussed at length. But no one came up with any good suggestions as to what could be done about Vester, because he really hadn't broken any laws. Tired and weary, everyone retired for the night.

Hildy lay awake a while trying to think what to do next. So far, all her plans had failed. She folded her hands across her chest, gazed up at the dark ceiling, and said a silent prayer. *Lord, I've done all I can think to do. I know it's your will that Iris have a home where somebody cares for her. And I know it's your will that Granny and Ruby's grandmother be reconciled. I've tried every plan I can think of. I've done all I can. Now, I'm asking you to do what I can't, and if it's your will, use me to make it happen. Amen.*

The next day, the little church was packed for the funeral service. Hildy sat down in front with Ruby, Uncle Nate, Seth, and Rachel. As Hildy stole a glance around, she saw that Ruby's grandmother was sitting near the front door, but she couldn't see her own grandmother anywhere. She was disappointed, but not really surprised.

After a neighbor woman sang "In the Garden," Nate rose, walked around the closed casket, and mounted the pulpit.

Even though Nate had only met the old preacher hours before his death, he'd learned a lot about Rufus Hurley from friends and neighbors. He gave a brief, moving account of the dead man's life as a servant of God in these hills.

"Now," Nate continued, "Brother Rufus didn't have much of this world's goods. He didn't even own the house in which he and his granddaughter, Iris, lived, but he was rich in friends who loved him."

Hildy glanced at Iris, who sat between two large women whom Hildy guessed were neighbors. She was surprised that Bertha hadn't come.

As her uncle continued to speak, Hildy looked quickly about the congregation again. *Granny's not coming*, she concluded. *Too bad!*

Focusing her attention on her uncle's words again, she heard, "It's always a sad time for folks when God calls one of his servants home, 'cause some folks got to stay here and hurt a spell. Like Iris, and y'all who knew this departed brother so well. But sometimes the Lord uses times of sadness like this to accomplish other things. I expect the good Lord's doin' those other things here today, though maybe you 'n' me don't know it.

"Now we're about to go to the gravesite for a final prayer. But I reckon it wouldn't be wrong of me to say that Brother Rufus had just arranged that I could preach here this Sunday. I'd sure be obliged if'n y'all came at eleven o'clock to hear what the Lord's a-givin' me to say then."

He paused, then lowered his voice. "It's about the liars and murderers in our midst."

Hildy heard a sharp intake of breath from the tightly packed congregation. She caught whispered words from the people sitting directly behind her, "Did he say 'murderers?' "

"And 'liars!' " someone whispered back.

Nate Konning went on with the service as though unaware of the electric current of interest his words had caused. He completed the ritual and directed the mourners to wait outside for the pallbearers at the gravesite.

As people filed out of the church, Hildy heard excited whispering everywhere.

Ruby sidled up to Hildy outside the front door. "Boy! Muh

daddy shore stirred up a powerful lot o' interest in his sermon! I reckon there ain't a single person here who'll stay away come Sunday."

Rachel nodded somberly. "Your father has a way of cutting right through to the heart of things. Seth and I'll be here for sure, won't we?" she said looking at her husband.

"Wild horses couldn't keep me away!" Seth replied. "Hmmm. Wonder how Nate got information in such a short time that we who've lived here for years don't know about."

Hildy had known her uncle for only a short while, but she knew him enough to realize he wasn't likely to tell her, or even Ruby, what he had in mind.

Ruby's father moved to the graveside and conducted the final ritual. When the brief prayer ended, Hildy found Ruby's grandmother.

The old woman stood at the back of the crowd, wearing a black dress that touched her shoes. Her black hat, long out of fashion, was secured with a single long hatpin that stuck out the front.

"Hello," Hildy said, uncertain of how the old woman would receive her.

"Hildy," she replied, the brim of her hat flopping forward as she nodded.

Hildy glanced back at Ruby just in time to see her turn quickly away. Then Hildy turned again to Mrs. Skaggs.

"Uh, too bad about Brother Hurley," Hildy said, not knowing what else to say.

"He was—" the old woman's voice broke, to Hildy's great surprise. "He was a good man," Mrs. Skaggs finished.

Hildy caught a glint of compassion in the old woman's eyes, revealing that she was genuinely touched. Hildy had pretty well decided earlier that nothing would soften this woman's hard heart, nor that of her own grandmother.

"I'm sure he was," Hildy replied.

There was a moment's awkward silence, then Ruby's grandmother spoke quietly, "He wasn't much older'n me. Shore makes a body think about things."

Then apparently deciding she'd said enough about that, she began to move away, saying, "I see somebody I got to speak with."

Puzzled about what was going through the old woman's mind, Hildy made her way back to Iris. She had walked away from the others and stood alone at the grave. The coffin had been lowered, and men were already filling the hole. The dirt fell with a sickening dull thud.

Iris whirled away, clapping both hands to her ears as though to blot out the sound. Her eyes were closed tightly, but tears seeped through and coursed down her cheeks.

"Iris," Hildy said softly, so as not to startle the girl, "Are you all right?"

She opened her eyes and reached out to her. "Oh, Hildy!" she whispered. "It hurts so much!"

Hildy hesitated for just a moment, as all the awful things Iris had said about her and all the mean things she had done flashed across Hildy's mind. Then she reached out and encircled Iris, pulling her close. "I know," Hildy whispered.

They held each other, gently rocking in silent grief. Hildy grieved not so much for the dead, as for this girl who now faced life without a living relative, a girl whose best friend had not even been present last night or at funeral.

Hildy wasn't sure how long she stood with her arms around Iris, but when she finally released her, Hildy felt different about the girl.

Iris looked steadily into Hildy's eyes. "What your uncle said about Gramps was nice, mighty nice."

Hildy nodded, not knowing how to answer the compliment.

Then Iris frowned. "But I wonder what he meant about comin' Sunday to hear about the liars and murderers?"

Hildy shrugged. "I honestly don't know. Guess all we can do is wait and see."

"I don't know about murderers," Iris shook her head, "but I got me some ideas about liars."

Hildy guessed that Iris referred to Bertha, because while she claimed to be Iris' friend, when she really needed one, Bertha hadn't been around.

"You got any ideas about who might be a murderer here-abouts?" Iris asked.

Hildy tried to not think of Vester, because she didn't really know the whole truth about him. She doubted anybody did. She said, "No, I don't. But I'm sure Uncle Nate wouldn't mention it if he couldn't prove it."

Iris managed a wan smile. "That's going to make it easier for me to live till Sunday." The smile vanished and she concluded, "After that, I don't know."

"It'll work out," Hildy said, feeling a twinge of guilt because everything she'd tried to do had failed.

"I hope so." Iris patted Hildy's arm. "Thanks for coming. And thanks for not holding the bad things I said and did to you and Ruby against me."

"It's all forgotten," Hildy replied, returning the pat.

Iris turned away. "See you Sunday then."

"Until Sunday," Hildy replied.

She could hardly wait, wondering what her uncle meant about liars and murderers.

One thing's for sure, Hildy told herself, *his sermon's certainly going to stir up trouble! Big trouble!*

CHAPTER
FIFTEEN

——

QUESTIONS ABOUT A
MYSTERY

By the next morning, word of Nate's sermon had already spread through the mountains. There was widespread speculation about who might be a murderer, and how could a newcomer like Nate Konning learn such a thing in a few days? The only possibility, it was decided, was that before the old preacher died, he had told Nate. In his upcoming sermon, Nate was going to reveal something to Possum Hollow that no other living person knew.

Hildy and Ruby, both in dresses but barefooted, picked up all this information shortly after Nate drove the rented horse and buggy into town and dropped the girls at the general store. He instructed them to approach everyone passing there and invite them to the Sunday service.

Ruby was glad to do that because it gave her an opportunity to let more people know that she had a father. He had caused quite a stir already, and Hildy guessed her cousin was feeling better about being a preacher's kid than she had been before.

Nate went calling house to house to invite people to the

service. At the same time, Seth and Rachel were calling in remote and isolated country areas where a stranger could get lost.

In less than an hour, word had spread that the girls were under the wooden overhang in front of Mr. Galvin's store. People found excuses to come there.

Sam Nayton was one of the first to tie his team in front of the store. Ruby whispered behind her hand, "Reckon his gossipy ol' missus heard jist enough to send him in to find out more. Lemme handle him."

Hildy was agreeable, so she stood back as the man in frayed overalls spat tobacco in the street and headed for the store door.

"Why, howdy, gals," he said, shifting the "chaw" to his left cheek. "Kinda surprised to see y'all here."

Ruby smiled warmly at the man. "We'uns come down to invite ever'body to hear muh daddy preach this Sunday. Come an' bring yore missus."

Sam shook his head sadly. "She's still mighty stove up with rheumatiz, so don't rightly 'spect she'll make it." He paused, then glanced around as if making sure nobody was close enough to overhear. "Ruby, I hear tell yore pa's a-gonna name some liars and murderers Sunday."

"That's what he said at the funeral."

Sam shifted his chewing tobacco again before lowering his voice and leaning close to Ruby. "I 'spect he done tol' ye who it is."

"No, he didn't. I almost begged him, bein' his daughter an' all, but he was tightmouthed as a snappin' turtle. He jist said, 'Ruby, honey, ye jist tell the folks to come to church next Lord's Day.' An' that's all he would say. Ain't that right, Hildy?"

When she nodded, Sam glanced nervously around again and motioned both girls to come closer. Hildy was reluctant, and stopped when she got an unpleasant whiff of the chewing tobacco on his breath.

He said in a hoarse whisper, "Ye reckon it's Vester? I mean, the murderer? Why, ever'body knows he's a liar, but he's not alone in that. Lots o' liars hereabouts. Howsomever, I'm proud to say I'm a truthful person."

Ruby said solemnly, "Jist like yore missus, huh?"

Hildy lowered her head to keep from letting a smile show at her cousin's jab at Mrs. Nayton's gossipy nature.

The man didn't seem to notice. "Yessiree! I betcha it's Vester! But who do ye think he murdered? An' how's he a-gonna take it when he finds out yore preacher daddy's a-gonna blab it to the whole wide world?"

Hildy swallowed hard and stepped back. She hadn't thought of that, but Vester certainly was the most likely person to be a murderer. If he was, and he thought the preacher was going to reveal that, Uncle Nate was in danger.

Hildy glanced at Ruby and realized from the look on her face that this was a new and terrible thought to her.

She said, "Mr. Nayton, I don't have the slightest idee who muh daddy's talkin' about. Y'all bring yore missus Sunday, and we'll all find out at the same time."

After he had gone, Hildy looked at Ruby in sudden concern. "I wonder if Uncle Nate thought of what that person or persons might do? Maybe we'd better go find him!"

The girls ran barefooted down the rocky street in the direction Nate had gone. After only half a block, Bertha and Elston came into sight.

Bertha broke into the mocking laughter Hildy knew so well. "Lookee here, Elston!" she said, stopping in the street with her bare feet wide apart.

Ruby's usual short temper did not flare up, as Hildy expected. Instead, her cousin said, "Mornin', Bertha, Elston. Good to see y'all. Hildy an' me want to invite ye to come hear muh daddy preach on Sunday."

Bertha's belligerent stance changed. She glanced at her companion, then back to Ruby and Hildy to ask, "Is it true what I heard he's gonna do?"

Ruby nodded. "Ye comin' to hear him?"

Bertha scowled and muttered, "I ain't been to church in a coon's age."

Barefooted Elston Edwards had not said anything. Hildy shifted her gaze to him and his mean brown eyes and shock of uncombed brown hair.

Ruby asked, "How about you, Elston?"

He smiled and parried her question with his own. "You be there?"

"Wouldn't miss it," Ruby assured him.

"Maybe the walls'll fall down or something," the boy replied, his smile widening, "but I'll be there!"

Hildy saw Bertha's mouth drop open in utter surprise. She turned to glare at the solid, muscular boy. "Ye never been inside no church! So why're ye—? Oh, I get it! Yo're going jist to see *her!*" Bertha shot a venomous glance at Ruby.

Elston shrugged. "So what if I am?" he said sharply. "It's no skin off your big nose!"

"Big nose?" Bertha exploded. "Why, I'll—!"

Hildy broke in. "Did either of you see my uncle? He was driving a sorrel gelding pulling a buggy."

Elston seemed glad for the interruption. "Parked down yonder," Elston said. "Come on, I'll show you!"

Hildy and Ruby walked on either side of the boy as he turned and led the away.

"I hope whoever the murderer is comes after y'all—includin' you, Elston!" Bertha yelled after them.

Hildy noticed that the boy laughed self-consciously at Bertha's threat, but he turned his full gaze upon Ruby. "I just can't get over the difference between you in a dress and in them boys' overalls you usually wear."

Ruby giggled, and Hildy dropped back a step and rolled her eyes. *I never thought I'd see the day Ruby'd giggle at some boy!* she mused.

They found Nate just as he was getting back into the buggy. It tipped sharply under his weight on the high step. When he saw the three approaching, he stepped back to the ground. "What's wrong?" he asked with a look of concern.

Hildy and Ruby quickly explained the fears Sam Nayton had aroused.

Nate stroked his clean-shaven chin. "I hadn't figured on anything like that. So I appreciate y'all a-comin' to warn me, but I reckon the good Lord'll take care of me. Now, y'all go back to the store and keep a-tellin' people. I'm a-gonna call on folks hereabouts."

On the way back to the store, Ruby kept looking back to where they'd left her father. "Shore hope he ain't a-gonna get hisself hurt," she said.

Elston tried to reassure her. "He'll be fine. But if it'd make you feel any better, Ruby, I could sort o' keep an eye on him."

"Would ye?" Ruby asked, giving the boy a grateful smile.

When Elston had turned back happily to follow Nate, Hildy and Ruby made their way back to the store. "You sure are changeable!" Hildy remarked.

Ruby grinned. "If'n I can protect muh daddy by givin' some ol' boy a smile, why not?"

"Bertha's probably in a stew about Elston going off with us like he did."

"So—what's she goin' to do about it?" Ruby demanded. "She'n me tangled afore, an' if she wants to try it again, I'll make her plumb sorry."

Hildy laughed. "In some ways you've changed, but in other ways, you're still the same old Ruby!"

Back in front of the general store, the cousins continued to invite all who passed by. And it seemed as if almost everyone in Possum Hollow found an excuse to stop by Mr. Galvin's for something or other.

Iris Hastings came along by midmorning. She approached them slowly, wearing a black dress that touched the tops of her bare feet. The three girls talked a while without bringing up the subject of her grandfather's death.

"When are you two figuring on going back to California?" Iris asked after some time.

"Daddy says him'n me got to leave Monday," Ruby said.

Iris looked at Hildy then, her eyes still red and puffy from crying. "I guess you're going too?"

Hildy hesitated, her mind filling with countless thoughts—mostly of Vester and Granny and what might happen if she were left alone in the Ozarks with them.

"I came to do some things," she said finally. "When I've done them, then I'll head back to California."

"Before you go," Iris said, reaching out to lightly touch Hildy's hand, "could—could—I talk with you alone?"

Hildy blinked in surprise. "Why, of course. You have time now?"

Ruby quickly agreed to stay and invite people to the service, so Hildy and Iris walked off together in the direction of the church.

"Ruby sure enjoys telling people about finding her father," Hildy commented.

"She's making them eat crow, all right!" Iris agreed. "I mean—she's lucky to have a father."

Hildy reached out and gave Iris' hand a gentle squeeze. "God is always there to help us through things. Of course, He expects us to do what we can, to do what's right. Just put your trust in Him, Iris, and He'll help you through this hard time."

"That's what Gramps used to say. But what makes you so sure that's true?"

"Oh, I see Him working in lives all the time, especially Ruby's and mine."

"Such as?"

"Well, I guess you heard about last June, when I came home and found my stepmother had moved away with my sisters and brother and I didn't know where they'd gone?"

"I heard that your grandmother had lied to your stepmother, causin' her to go off and leave you behind."

"That was a terrible time for me," Hildy recalled, her voice sad with the memory. Then she brightened. "But look at how it all worked out. When Ruby and I ran away, Granny sent Vester to bring us back. While we were running, Ruby and I met Seth and Rachel. We also met some wonderful people in Oklahoma who gave us the first clue that helped us find Ruby's father.

"Then after Vester had kidnapped Ruby and me, and before the police caught him, we met Spud, and we escaped and found my parents who took us to California."

"Who's Spud?"

Hildy's thoughts flashed back to the freckled boy with the

green eyes. "Oh, he's just a boy I know."

"Where is he now?"

"Back with his parents in New York." Hildy didn't want to say anymore about Spud because he was someone special to her. So she switched the subject: "I also saw God working in Ruby's life. As you know, for years she thought her father was dead. But step by step we were led to him. Ruby was dying to get back here and show him off to everybody."

The girls turned into the churchyard toward some shade trees.

Iris mused aloud, "I guess she's got a right to be bragging about him and introducing him to everybody. I just wish I had somebody. I hate being alone! Maybe that's why I'm so mad at Gramps for dying!"

Hildy was startled. "You don't mean that!"

"No, I guess not. Truth is, Hildy, I'm so mixed up! At first, I couldn't believe he was dead. Then I got mad at him, and that makes me feel terrible guilty inside."

"I felt that way once in California about a really good friend I had named Twyla. Her folks were so poor they had to—to—" Hildy's voice faltered. "They had to give all her brothers and sisters away to strangers, and finally they gave Twyla away, too."

"That's awful! I remember Gramps reading to me once from the paper about that happening to some folks."

"To me," Hildy continued, "losing Twyla was like having someone die. At first, I couldn't believe it happened. Then I got mad, then I felt guilty, and finally—finally, I accepted it."

"You mean—that's what a person has to go through before they can go on with their life?"

Hildy nodded and then held Iris' eyes in a firm gaze. "But there's one thing I haven't accepted," she said quietly. "It's the way my grandmother has acted toward me. And the way Ruby's grandmother has been toward Ruby. The more I think about you, the more I—" Her voice trailed off, and she looked up toward the surrounding mountains.

"What?" Iris prompted.

"—the more I'm determined to do what I came here to do

before I go back to California," Hildy finished.

"I heard that your grandmother, with Vester's help, is not going to let you go back. But they can't stop you if you go with Ruby and her father!" Iris paused, then added in a low voice, "I heard that Vester might be the one your uncle mentioned as bein' a murderer. If he is, well, maybe neither Ruby or you will ever get back to California."

A cold chill rippled through Hildy. *Granny's in danger too!* she thought. *But she's also the one person who could clear up this whole problem!*

Hildy turned abruptly to Iris and said, "I've got to see my grandmother right away. But—are you going to be all right now?"

"I'll be fine. I just needed to talk to someone. Thanks, Hildy. You're a friend."

Hildy brightened at the comment. "Will you tell Ruby where I've gone?"

"Sure—but watch out for Vester!"

"I think I'll be all right in broad daylight."

Hildy felt sure about her own safety, but not about Granny's. She was all alone, away off in the wooded mountains. Vester could carry out his threat against Granny anytime. Hildy hurried down the road.

CHAPTER SIXTEEN

TROUBLE AT THE CHURCH

Granny Dunnigan sat in her hickory rocking chair and vigorously puffed on her corncob pipe while Hildy talked. When she was finished, Granny pulled the old pipe from her mouth and waved it in the air. "Ye got a powerful lot o' wants today, Hildy. Let's see. Ye want me to come to church Sunday, and make up with muh no-'count sister, an' tell Vester they ain't no hex on him, an'—" She paused to think.

Hildy jumped in, "And consider taking Iris in to live with you, and say you forgive me and really understand why I ran off last summer. Oh, and promise you won't try to stop me from going back home, and you won't let Vester do it either."

Granny took another puff on the foul-smelling pipe and blew smoke at the ceiling before answering, "Even in fairytales a body gener'ly gets only three wishes. But ye want more."

"They're all important, Granny. And you can do all of them."

"I cain't force Gussie to make up with me, even if I wanted to."

"You could try, Granny!"

135

"Why should I? Let her take the first step. She started it all!"

"What'd she do?"

Granny frowned, puffing thoughtfully on the pipe. "Never mind," she said finally.

Hildy tried a bold move. "You don't really remember what it was about, do you?"

" 'Course I do! When we was girls, we was close as peas in a pod. Lived together till we got married. Then one time, she—uh—I don't want to talk about it."

"Okay, but you could do all the other things I asked. You can forgive me for running off and say you really understand that my place is with my own family."

"Hildy, yo're all the family I got. If'n ye stay here, I'll give ye everything a gal your age could want." Granny's voice softened. "I got a lot o' love to give somebody, but when I cain't, it sort of sours inside and makes me do selfish an' mean things."

"Granny, I love you, and I'd like to stay here, but I can't. There are other choices for you."

Granny didn't reply. Instead, she reached down and lifted her long, dark skirt above her ankles. Hildy saw an ugly, black bruise.

"What happened?" she cried, bending to get a closer look.

"Like to a-fell into the well fetching water. But it wasn't no accident. No, siree! Somebody done stretched wahr at the curb."

"Was it Vester?"

"Had to be him. Since I'm half blind, I didn't see the wahr, an' tripped. Mighta fell in, head first, only I grabbed the rope and ketched muh balance."

"Oh, Granny, he might try again unless you tell him there's no hex on him!"

"He most likely will try, but I ain't a-gonna tell him they ain't really no hex."

Hildy saw that there was no reasoning with her hardheaded grandmother on the subject, so she went on to another: "I wonder what makes Vester so mean?"

"I know why, 'cause I knowed his pa—Troy Hardesty by name. He was a strict, hardshell preacher spoutin' fire 'n' brimstone. Only thing is, he didn't practice what he preached. Had no more love for his boy than a snake for a baby chick.

"Troy beat Vester reg'lar when he was jist a mite of a boy. Then he'd brag to everybody that he was jist a-followin' the Good Book 'bout the danger of sparin' the rod and spoilin' the child, but I knowed better'n that. Troy had a mean streak in 'im. He jist needed an excuse to whup the boy on accounta his own life wasn't good. Jist between you an' me, I seen that preacher a-swiggin' outta a jug! Others seen him doin' other things a man o' the cloth ought not to be doin'.

"In fact, the man was so mean-tempered he run his own wife off when Vester was about twelve, and half-growed. Them two got into it, an' Vester tried to fight his pa, but he wasn't big enough o' course, so he ran away too."

Granny stopped and regarded the bowl of her pipe a moment before continuing. "Some coon hunters found Troy's body a few days later. Sheriff said it looked like Troy was a-sittin' up on them sandstone ridges an' fell off."

Hildy nodded. "I know those cliffs."

Granny concluded, "Sheriff said it was an accident, but lots o' folks hereabouts don't think so. They figger he was pushed."

"Oh, Granny! How awful!"

In spite of her feelings of revulsion toward the bearded, pockfaced moonshiner, Hildy felt some stirring of sympathy and understanding for Vester. At the same time, she felt deep concern for what Vester could do to herself and the people she loved.

Granny went on, "Vester tol' me once that he hates religion, so he turned to superstition an' hexes."

Hildy wondered how Granny could claim to be a Christian and yet dabble in superstition and threaten people with hexes, but she was reluctant to ask.

"I ain't got much left in this world, Hildy," Granny explained, " 'ceptin' the power I got over some people on accounta what *they* believe I kin do. Like Vester."

Hildy didn't understand why anyone would want power over someone, but she realized her grandmother had told her the truth. Then she pleaded, "Please, Granny, just tell Vester that you don't really have a hex on him, so he'll leave you alone!"

"I ain't a-gonna do it! And I don't wanna hear no more about it!"

Hildy's strong will surged to the surface. "Are you doing this so I won't leave?"

"I don't know what yo're a-talkin' about!" Granny answered craftily.

"You think I'm too frightened to leave while your life's in danger. You think I can't leave you alone while your health's poor, and your eyesight's getting worse. You're counting on all those things to keep me here, aren't you?"

Granny puffed silently on her pipe without looking up.

Hildy was becoming increasingly upset, terrified that she would not be able to work things out after all. Her conscience wouldn't allow her go off and leave Granny under the circumstances. But to be separated from her family—she couldn't face that either.

"I'm going outside to think," she announced.

"While yo're out there, would ye mind feedin' the chickens and sloppin' the hog?"

Hildy detected a note of triumph in her grandmother's voice. It was as though with that simple question, Granny knew she had won. Hildy would not leave the Ozarks.

Sick at heart, Hildy carried out her grandmother's instructions. She was trapped, frustrated, and angry. Besides praying, there was only one other thing she could do.

I won't tell Ruby, Hildy decided. *No sense upsetting her. She's having too good a time showing off her father.*

Just as Hildy turned away from feeding the hog, she caught a glimpse of Vester disappearing into the woods.

He's watching us! she thought, her heart racing with fear. *It's just a matter of time until he does something terrible—if he catches one of us alone.* Hildy shivered in spite of the hot, muggy day.

Hildy didn't really want to stay with her grandmother all the time. She didn't like being outfoxed and feeling trapped. But her conscience wouldn't let her leave the old woman alone either. So Hildy resolved to stay with her grandmother through the next two days and nights.

Granny was soft-spoken and pleasant throughout the time. But she dropped things, claiming she couldn't close her hands around anything because of arthritis. She bumped into furniture and doorjambs, complaining she couldn't see. Three times in Hildy's presence, she tripped and almost fell.

I think she's doing all this just to play on my sympathy and make me stay here, Hildy thought. *But I can't be sure. It's a cinch she needs somebody to look after her, but I'm not the one to do it, am I?*

Hildy was feeling more and more guilty about leaving Granny. So far, everything she'd tried had failed, and time was running out. She'd either have to return to California, or give up and stay here.

She silently prayed, repeating over and over, *Lord, I've done all I can! I need your help, and soon!*

As Sunday morning dawned, Hildy climbed down from the loft in Granny's log house. Granny was just retrieving her false teeth from the glass by her bed.

Hildy asked, "Are you sure you won't change your mind and go with us today? I'd like to sit with you in church."

"I been a-thinkin' on it. If'n I knew Gussie wouldn't be thar, I might jist go."

"I hope she *is* there," Hildy said, splashing cool water on her face and drying it with the rag-towel on the nail hook.

"If'n she is, I'm a-leavin'! All thar is to it."

"But you *will* go?"

"We'll see," Granny replied.

A little later, Seth and Rachel arrived with a team pulling a spring wagon. They had placed empty boxes in the back to serve as seats for Hildy and Granny.

Reluctantly, the old woman shuffled out of the house in a somber, black dress that covered her from the throat to her wrists, and down to her ankles. She wore a plain, black straw hat, brightened a bit with a clump of red cherries on the brim. Hildy had never before seen the plain black shoes that her grandmother wore today. They didn't have cut-outs for her toes as the others did.

Hildy felt happy as they rode into town, grateful that her grandmother was going to church. Yet she also had a sense of anxiety. She wasn't sure if it was because of the subject of Uncle Nate's sermon, or if it was something else.

When they arrived, the churchyard was already packed with buggies, wagons, and a few saddle horses. Hildy was surprised to see Elston dressed in clean pants and a short-sleeved shirt, even though he was obviously quite uncomfortable. She noticed him watching Ruby as she and her father arrived in their rented buggy. As Granny stopped to speak with another older woman, Hildy joined Seth and Rachel as they met up with Ruby and Nate.

"Ruby, I've never seen you looking so good!" Hildy exclaimed. "What a pretty dress! And that hat!"

Even though it was a plain gray, the dress somehow looked cheerful on Ruby. "It was an ol' one o' Rachel's," Ruby explained. "She took a few tucks here an' thar to make it fit. And she loaned me the hat."

They were soon interrupted by several townspeople who came up to Ruby and her father to greet them. Hildy detected both respect and curiosity in their greetings. "People are sure anxious to hear your father expose liars and murderers today," Hildy whispered to Ruby when the adults were taken up in other conversation. "But I think Elston came just to see you."

Ruby self-consciously fingered the ribbon on her straw hat. "Aw, he didn't neither!" But at the same time, she glanced at Elston and smiled.

Hildy directed her attention to the church entrance and saw Iris standing alone on the steps. It made her wonder again where Bertha was. Then she turned to her grandmother who had joined them, "Would you mind if I asked Iris to sit with us, Granny?"

"Don't matter none to me. But I know what yo're up to, Hildy Corrigan, and it ain't a-gonna do ye no good."

Even though everyone in Possum Hollow knew everyone else, Hildy made a point of introducing her grandmother to Iris. She gratefully accepted Hildy's invitation to sit with them.

As they started inside together, Hildy asked Iris, "Have you seen Bertha?"

"Not since Gramps died," Iris replied with a painful look. "Fine friend she turned out to be, huh?"

"Don't be too hard on her," Hildy replied. "Some people don't know what to say when someone has died."

Iris snapped, "She didn't need to *say* anything. She could have just been there! Like you were, Hildy. Even though you had every reason in the world to stay away from me."

An usher motioned for them to follow. As they passed an open window, Hildy caught a glimpse of Vester leaning against a wheel of Uncle Nate's buggy. Hildy felt a sudden surge of alarm. Then she reassured herself, *He wouldn't try anything with all these people around!*

The church was already packed, and the three were led to seats in the front row. Hildy sat between Granny and Iris. She wanted to tell Ruby that Vester was outside, but her cousin was already seated with Seth and Rachel in the center of a pew half-way back.

Nate Konning entered from a door on Hildy's right where she assumed the pastor's study was located. The visiting preacher climbed the two steps to the pulpit area and took a straight-backed chair, while Mr. Galvin stood to lead the singing.

When he asked the congregation to join him in standing, Hildy turned her head toward the front door. She half expected to see Vester, but instead Ruby's grandmother walked in, leaning on the arm of an usher. He seated her in the last row near the door.

Hildy was so excited she tried to get Ruby's attention, but her cousin didn't understand her motions. As the singing began in earnest, Granny gently elbowed her granddaughter to indicate her displeasure at such inappropriate behavior.

Hildy fought the rising sense of doom within her by singing loudly with the congregation, "Onward, Christian Soldiers." Iris didn't open her mouth, but Granny surprised Hildy by joining in with enthusiasm.

They were on the second verse when an usher came down

the aisle and motioned for Nate. He walked across the platform and bent down to hear the man's whispered message. Nate nodded and relayed something to Mr. Galvin, who was leading the singing with gusto.

Where's he going? Hildy wondered, as her uncle left the platform and went out the back door.

Then she remembered who was standing outside, and screamed a warning in her mind, *Vester's out there! Don't go out alone, Uncle Nate!* She turned to Granny for permission to be excused, but her grandmother shook her head and held her arm.

Hildy turned around and was surprised to see every eye focused on the back door. Ruby started rise, but Rachel seemed to restrain her. Ruby nodded and continued singing.

Nate had not returned by the time the now-seated congregation was singing the last verse of the second hymn, "Amazing Grace." Hildy was becoming more and more concerned about her uncle. When she glanced back at Ruby again she saw her tug at Seth's sleeve. He listened while Ruby whispered something to him. Then he nodded, spoke briefly to Rachel, and left by the outside aisle toward the back door, with Ruby following.

Before they could reach it, the door opened, and a small gasp rose from the congregation.

Nate's suit was rumpled as though he'd been in a scuffle, and the right sleeve was split at the shoulder seam. His hair was tousled, and he bore a small cut on his lower lip and a bruise under one eye.

Mr. Galvin's arms dropped at the sight, and the congregation broke off the singing by fragments.

Hildy watched helplessly as Seth and Ruby rushed up to Nate. They exchanged a few anxious words before Seth returned to his seat. Nate held his daughter in his arms for a moment before gently guiding her back toward her seat.

There was total silence in the tiny church as Nate mounted the steps to the platform again, motioned for the song leader to sit down, and took the pulpit.

"Reckon the good Lord won't mind if we don't sing any more just now. May's well start my sermon. I thank ye all kindly for comin', and I'll try to say something that will make a difference in everyone of your lives."

He gently touched his cut lip, then glanced at his fingers. "A Philistine feller outside was a-tryin' to take my buggy wheels off. I discouraged him a mite, but he resisted. After turning both cheeks, I smote him."

Hildy whispered to Granny, "It was Vester!"

"That preacher's got grit!" She said with obvious approval.

Nate continued, "The way I figure it, I have a command from God to speak the gospel truth today, no matter what happens. An' that's exactly what I'm a-gonna do."

He paused, and Hildy sensed the electric tension in the room. She watched in fascination as her uncle gazed silently around the congregation. Finally, he spoke.

"I see we've got some liars among us."

Hildy heard the sharp intake of breath from the packed body of mountain folk.

Nate looked around the room again. "I also see we got us a murderer or two with us."

This time, the collective gasp was so audible that Hildy glanced around. Everyone else seemed to be doing the same thing, wondering who the preacher meant.

Nate's voice boomed out, strong and firm. "Now, if y'all would bow your heads, I'm gonna ask the Lord's blessin' on the preachin'. Then I'm gonna let go with what I have to say!"

Hildy's heart was beating hard with excitement and anticipation. She was sure everybody present was wondering with her: *Who are the liars? Who are the murderers?*

Knowing her uncle, he wouldn't purposely incite a riot, but then what *would* happen? Hildy could hardly wait for the sermon to start.

CHAPTER
SEVENTEEN

—

A TERRIBLE SURPRISE

Nate prayed briefly and opened his Bible. Then he stepped out from behind the pulpit so there was nothing between him and the people. As he gazed silently across the congregation for what seemed a long time, Hildy thought he had probably looked every single person in the eye.

His first words were blunt. "Any liars here today?" He paused, then raised his voice slightly. "Anybody in this room a murderer?"

The girl heard the stirring and whispering around her as Nate put his finger on the passage and read aloud.

"In First John, four and twenty, it says, 'If a man say, I love God, and hateth his brother, he is a liar: for he that loveth not his brother whom he hath seen, how can he love God whom he hath not seen?' "

Nate raised his eyes and swept the congregation again. "That's the first part o' my text. The second part is from One John three and fifteen." He lowered his eyes and ran his fingers along the words. "Whosoever hateth his brother is a murderer: and ye know that no murderer hath eternal life abiding in him."

Nate's voice rose slightly each time he said the word 'murderer.' Hildy felt tense as her uncle lowered the Bible. His left eye was swelling noticeably, and Hildy guessed it would be closed by the end of the sermon.

"I got the feelin' some of ye came today thinkin' I might be gonna preach about some other feller's sin," Nate said with a faint smile. "Well, I ain't a-gonna do that. My job is to preach the gospel. The Holy Spirit's job is to convict guilty folks, including those denying they're liars and murderers, even tellin' themselves they aren't."

Hildy sensed that people were disappointed the visiting preacher wasn't going to reveal the name of some unknown murderer, but her uncle didn't seem concerned about that.

He continued, "So I ask y'all again: Are there any liars in the church today? Are there any murderers here? Now, don't ye go a-lookin' 'round and thinkin' about that other brother or sister. Just look deep inside your own soul and tell God—don't tell me—the answer to these questions."

An uneasy stillness settled over the congregation. Hildy could feel it. She also suspected that the barbed words pricked the hearts and consciences of many people, including her own grandmother and Ruby's grandmother. But how would they take the words of a visiting preacher, even if they *were* words from the Bible itself?

Hildy fought a strong desire to look at her grandmother, sitting next to her, but she was afraid to be so obvious. She also feared Granny might go into one of her contrary spells and yell out at the preacher.

But Hildy couldn't resist turning her head ever so slowly and stealing a glance at Ruby's grandmother, seated in the back. Grandma Skaggs' face was hard as granite and her expression cold as steel.

As Hildy let her gaze sweep around, it fell on Ruby, who raised her eyebrows slightly to acknowledge that she saw her cousin. Then, as though wondering why Hildy was looking at the back of the church, Ruby also turned. She stiffened instantly in surprise.

Hildy was sure then that Ruby had not known her grandmother was in the congregation. Hildy's head was still turned to the back when Granny elbowed her in the ribs, and she returned her attention to the pulpit.

Uncle Nate continued, his open Bible secured in his left hand. "Now some of ye may be asking yourselves, 'Why should I be concerned?' So lemme give y'all a third verse."

He quickly turned to another page and announced, "In Matthew the sixth chapter, the fourteenth and fifteenth verses, it says, 'For if ye forgive men their trespasses, your heavenly Father will also forgive you: But if ye forgive not men their trespasses, neither will your Father forgive your trespasses.' "

Hildy heard a stirring again amongst the people as Nate paused, then added with a wan smile, "After that sinner outside whupped me in the mouth, an' in the eye," he gingerly touched the bruise under his left eye, "I tol' him I forgave him for smitin' me, an' then I asked the Lord to forgive him *and* me."

In his slow drawl and deliberate speech, Nate spoke about each of the three Bible verses, illustrating each point with stories about people he'd known in his native Texas and in California, where he now lived.

Hildy watched with growing concern as her uncle's eye swelled nearly shut and his lips puffed up. By the time he neared the end of his sermon, his speech was slurred.

"Now I got to ask y'all one more time, an' then I'm done. Are there any liars in this church today? Are there any murderers here? If there are, then ye know what to do, 'cause the Bible tells you flat out.

"Get up out of your seat and make up with your brother, your sister now. Why, you say? For the best reason in the world. The Scriptures make it plain as the nose on your face! The Lord won't forgive ye 'less'n ye first forgive others.

"Now, don't go a-blamin' the other feller, 'cause the Bible don't say to do that! God's Word don't say nothin' about who's to blame. Ye got no cause to say, 'It's his fault, or it's her fault!' No siree! God don't say nothin' 'bout blame, and he don't say nothin' 'bout excuses!

"Only one thing matters: whether you're guilty or not guilty.

So if'n you're guilty, make it right with your brother or your sister here'n now. Then come down here to this altar and make it right with the Lord. If ye need help, I'm here for that.

"Don't get me wrong, ye don't have to answer to me, but ye do have to answer to the Lord—sooner or later. It's your choice. Now, what are ye a-gonna do about it?"

Nate closed his Bible and walked down the few steps to stand expectantly behind the altar.

Hildy still hesitated to look at her grandmother, sensing that she was puffed up, about to explode. Hildy hoped Granny wouldn't make a scene.

Mr. Galvin arose and asked everyone to stand and sing, "Just As I Am." As Hildy stood with the others, she couldn't stifle the temptation to look back at Ruby's grandmother. Grandma Skaggs stood perfectly straight—rigid, tense, filled with anger. She seemed to glower at the preacher, who stood alone behind the altar.

Just then Hildy felt her own grandmother twist around to see what had attracted her attention. Ruby's grandmother lowered her eyes from Nate's and met her sister's.

"Oh!" Granny gasped in obvious surprise.

Hildy realized it was the first time her grandmother knew that her sister was present.

The two old sisters glared at each other in open hostility. Hildy felt sad, realizing her uncle's sermon had not touched the two old women. On the contrary, they seemed more stiff-necked than ever.

Some, however, had been moved. They began moving out of the aisles, tearfully seeking others.

The plaintive words of the old hymn filled the air. "O Lamb of God, I come, I come."

Hildy turned around at Iris' touch. There were tears in her eyes as she gripped Hildy's hands hard. "Oh, Hildy! I never realized *all* the bad things Bertha an' me did to you till now! And you've been so nice to me, in spite of that, since Gramps died! Forgive me, please?"

"Of course I do!" Hildy said, leaning close.

Iris sniffed, a tear sliding down her cheek. "I need to go to the altar an' ask God to forgive me, too."

Hildy nodded and started to free her hands, but Iris whispered urgently. "Come with me? Please?"

Other people started forward as Hildy turned to her grandmother. "Iris wants me to go to the altar with her."

Granny nodded, her face stiff as a frozen pond.

Hildy took a deep breath, wondering if she dared make a suggestion when Granny was obviously angry. But she decided to try. "Granny, why don't you go talk to your sister?"

Granny's dark eyes snapped in the same way Hildy had seen so often before. "I know what yo're a-tryin' to do, Hildy, an' it won't work! *She* started this! Let her come to *me*!"

Hildy drew back, rebuffed at Granny's sharp tone. Turning again to the back of the room, she saw Ruby leaning toward her grandmother and speaking to her. Then Ruby straightened, met Hildy's eyes, and shrugged. Ruby's grandmother stared stonily ahead at the preacher, who was helping people who had come to kneel at the altar.

Slowly, Hildy sighed and nodded in understanding. *It's useless*, she thought. *They're never going to make up!* "Let's go, Iris," she said softly.

The altar was so full that Hildy led Iris around to the pastor's side. The two girls knelt together, and Hildy placed her arm around Iris' shoulders. Bending forward, her face almost touched the altar.

After some time, Hildy raised her eyes to see that almost everyone had left the church. Hildy's grandmother was shuffling out the front door, while her sister left by the side door.

I've failed again! Hildy thought, fighting tears. *And my prayers weren't answered either! That hurts more than anything.*

She glanced at her uncle, who knelt beside a man at the altar. Hildy could see the pride in Ruby's shining eyes as she stood next to her father. *It must be wonderful to know that your father is making such a difference in people's lives*, Hildy thought.

She and Iris walked arm in arm out of the church. When they got outside, Iris looked up and exclaimed, "Hey! It's a-cloudin' up! Maybe it's finally gonna rain!"

"Looks like there's a storm moving in fast, all right. See the lightning in the distance?"

"Sure hope it's a good soaker!" Iris declared. "I ain't never seen the woods so dry!"

Hildy nodded and looked around the grounds. She saw her grandmother, Seth, and Rachel talking beside the spring wagon. She continued to search the churchyard, not really expecting to see Vester, but at the same time, wondering where he was. He was nowhere in sight, but she did notice Bertha and Elston standing in the shadow of the church. Hildy had not seen Bertha before now.

Three older women drew Iris aside. Hildy began to walk toward her grandmother, until Elston intercepted her. She could hear Bertha's disapproving comment, but Elston ignored her.

"Hildy, I—well," he began, "I'm sorry for the things I did to you and Ruby when you lived here."

Hildy waited, but realized Elston couldn't quite bring himself to ask forgiveness. Hildy smiled at him. "It's all right, Elston."

The boy nodded his thanks and turned away, then swung back and lowered his voice, "Vester's gone now, but he's been watching everything from the woods. Probably up to no good."

Hildy realized Elston didn't know Vester was the one who had fought with her uncle. She guessed that he had not fared well in the brief encounter, and he would likely be even more angry—and more dangerous.

Is he waiting to catch Uncle Nate again? she wondered, then shook her head. *No, not with Seth around. But maybe he's after Granny or Ruby—or me.*

Hildy continued on to the wagon. Looking at her grandmother, she thought of the few words that would solve most of Hildy's problems, if only Granny would say them. But she was too stubborn for that.

"Hildy, I was just telling your grandmother how brave your uncle was to preach a sermon like that," Rachel said.

"Humph!" Granny grunted with disapproval. "He started off preachin' real good, then he went to meddlin'."

"But, Granny, you said he had grit!"

"I spoke too soon, Hildy. I'll be one glad woman when he's gone back to Californy."

Seth raised an eyebrow. "Maybe he won't go. I just overheard a couple of them elders or deacons a-talkin'. They was sayin' as how they'd like to ask Nate to stay on and be the reg'lar preacher."

Hildy exclaimed, "Really? Is that true?"

"Gospel truth," Seth replied.

Hildy looked around for Ruby, then turned back to Seth. "Does Ruby know?"

Seth shrugged. "I don't know, but it's a sure thing Nate don't yet, 'cause he's still inside the church. Besides, I figure them fellers won't say nothin' to Nate until they meet this afternoon and discuss it, legal-like. Leastwise, that's what I heard one of 'em say."

Hildy's mind took a plunge at this unexpected news. *If the church calls Uncle Nate, and he accepts, then he and Ruby would have to stay here in the Ozarks*, she thought. *But what does that mean for me?*

"I've got to talk to Ruby!" she announced abruptly. She ran across the churchyard and into the building. Uncle Nate was still standing at the altar, counseling a man, but Ruby was gone.

Hildy saw Mr. Galvin talking to a small group near the side door. She hurried over. "Excuse me, Mr. Galvin, but did you see where Ruby went?"

"Why, yes. She went out this door a couple of minutes ago."

"Thanks!" Hildy said, and started out the door.

The merchant added, "Right after I told her the church board was thinking of calling her father as our regular preacher."

"What?" Hildy exclaimed in alarm. She dashed out the door just as distant thunder boomed, and lightning flashed across the threatening sky.

Elston called out to her, "If you're looking for Ruby, she just ran into the woods." He pointed, adding, "Said something about having to get away and think."

"Elston, would you tell my grandmother I'm going after Ruby?"

"Okay," he replied, "but you'd better hurry, or you'll both get caught in the rain."

Hildy ran for the tinder-dry forest as lightning flashed again and thunder cracked.

Completely forgetting that the angry, vengeful Vester might be waiting there, she dashed through the woods in search of her cousin.

CHAPTER
EIGHTEEN

INTO THE FLAMING
TRAP

Hildy was about a hundred yards into the densely-wooded hillside before she remembered Vester. She glanced back anxiously, but saw no one. "Ruby! Ruby, where are you?" she called.

Lightning split the sky, followed by a clap of thunder. But there was no answer from her cousin.

Hildy ran on, breathing hard, climbing up the steep mountainside, yelling Ruby's name. At the same time, Hildy looked back with a silent prayer, *O Lord, don't let Vester find her!*

At the top of a small hill, Hildy jumped up on an old tree stump and looked in all directions. "There you are!" she cried aloud.

Hildy leaped down and darted around trees to where she'd seen Ruby trudging up a steep hill. She soon caught up with her, winded but relieved. "Where're you going?" she asked.

"Jist a-walkin'. Oh, Hildy, didja hear what they're a-gonna do?"

Hildy nodded. "But maybe they'll change their minds, or if

they do offer him the job, maybe he won't accept it!"

"It was jist such a turrible surprise I had to get away an' think."

"Well, this is about as far as you'd better go." Hildy cocked an anxious eye at the glowering sky. "Looks like it's going to rain cats and dogs pretty soon."

Another lightning flash made Hildy cringe. She knew that a strike in this dry forest could start a wildfire. She shook off the thought and looked at her cousin.

"Elston said Vester was watching when church let out, but he disappeared into these woods, so we'd better get back."

"Soon's I kin catch muh breath."

"You want to sit down a bit and talk?" Hildy asked.

Ruby shrugged, carefully arranged her Sunday dress, and gingerly sat down on a fallen log. Hildy sat down too, waiting for Ruby to speak first.

Still breathing a little hard from the climb, Ruby began, "I cain't bear to think o' bein' separated from ye, Hildy. But he's muh daddy, so no matter what he does, I reckon I'll stay with him."

"I understand, but I never thought I'd hear you say that."

"Ye think I'm wrong?"

"Oh, no!" Hildy shook her head, sending her brown braids flipping wildly. "Your place is with your father. I just meant that I never thought you'd want to stay here in the Ozarks—for any reason."

"Ain't muh choice, ye know. Reckon they's no place I like well's Californy. But if'n Daddy stays, I stay."

Hildy wondered if she should tell Ruby that she might also have to stay here because of Granny. *Not yet*, she told herself. *We need to get out of these woods before Vester comes, or we'll get soaked by the rain*, she thought, not wanting to alarm Ruby.

"You're right, of course, about staying if your daddy stays," Hildy said. "But I just hate the thought of us ever being sepa-rated."

"Me, too." Ruby's voice was soft and filled with pain. Then she brightened. "Anyways, we'd all have to go back to Californy first. Daddy's got to get that bull out to Lone River for Mr. Farnham, and I got to he'p his wife on the train. Ye got to take keer of them little kids, Hildy. I reckon muh daddy an' me'd jist have to come back here soon's we could."

Both girls looked up as a jagged streak of lightning lit up the sky. It was so close that Hildy began judging its distance by counting to herself, *One Mississippi, two Mississippi, three Miss*— she broke off as a thunder clap crashed around them.

"Boy!" Hildy cried, jumping up and glancing around at the menacing sky. "That was close!"

"An' comin' closer!" Ruby leaped to her feet and brushed the back of her dress. "We'uns better get back!"

The cousins began running as fast as they dared down the steep wooded mountain while thunder and lightning split the sky on all sides. Hildy was not usually afraid of lightning, but since her horse had been struck while she was riding in Oklahoma this summer, she was much more wary of storms.

Ruby panted as they ran side by side, "If'n Daddy an' me come back here to live, ye reckon ye would too?"

Hildy kept thinking as she ran that she probably should tell Ruby about what had happened at Granny's since the girls had last seen each other.

But before Hildy could answer, Ruby spoke again, "Maybe that's what yo're supposed to do, Hildy! If'n ye stay here, yore granny's goin' to be happy, an' Vester'd leave us alone."

Hildy slid to a stop and grabbed her cousin's arm. "You know, I saw Vester outside the church just before the service started. I'm sure he's the one who gave your father that black eye and cut lip. Then Elston saw him again right after the service, so maybe—"

Ruby spun anxiously in all directions. "Ye reckon he'd bother us in daylight?"

"Well, we *are* alone out here in the woods." Just then there was another lightning bolt and a clap of thunder, accompanied by an explosion just over the ridge behind them.

"That one hit something!" Hildy cried. "Tree, most likely. Could start a fire, too. Let's get out of here!"

She bolted to run, but Ruby pulled on her hand. "We'uns could be a-runnin' straight into Vester! I mean, if'n he was a-follerin' us, an' we go back the same way we come up."

"You're right!" Hildy said, peering ahead into the shadows. "Let's circle around to the left and get to the church that way."

After only a few hundred yards, Hildy stopped and sniffed. "I smell smoke!" She turned to look back the way they'd come. "Look!" She pointed to flames just beginning to leap up from the tree struck by lightning.

"Let's hurry!" Ruby cried, starting down the hill again. Then she pulled to a halt. "Oh-oh!"

There before them, not a hundred feet away, stood Vester, his legs spread apart in a defiant stance.

"Whoa thar!" he called, rolling a kitchen match in the corner of his mouth. "Not so fast. Don't you wanna stop and talk a spell?" He grinned, showing yellow, tobacco-stained teeth.

"Get outta our way!" Ruby yelled.

"Now, that ain't nice, Ruby," he said menacingly, stroking his reddish-brown beard. "Tell ye what. They's a little cave over yonder a piece." He waved vaguely to his side. "Big enough for all o' us to get in outta the rain."

"It ain't rainin'!" Ruby snapped. "Are ye gonna get outta the way, or not?"

Hildy grabbed her hot-tempered cousin's hand and whispered, "There's no use talking to him! Let's circle off to the right and go around him."

As the girls started to move that way, Vester called, "Now, now. Ye cain't get by me. I kin cut ye off, and ye know it."

"Let's go back!" Ruby whispered.

Hildy glanced over her shoulder. "Can't! The whole mountain is on fire!"

The girls looked at each other, then at Vester.

He rolled the match to the other corner of his mouth and called, "Ye comin' to the cave or not?"

"No!" Ruby yelled defiantly.

"Shhh!" Hildy hissed under her breath. "Don't make him mad!"

"Suit yoreselves!" Vester reached for the match and struck it with his thumbnail. It flared into life. "Last chance, girls!"

They stood uncertainly as the match burned high in the man's hand. Then, very deliberately, he stooped down and held the match to the dry brush at his feet. A curl of smoke rose, followed by small flames that snapped and crackled.

"What's he a-doin'?" Ruby whispered.

"Cutting us off!" Hildy replied, fear edging her voice. She glanced around. The sky was already bright with flames leaping to other trees and making a roaring sound.

Hildy turned back to her cousin. "We can either go right or left, but I don't know this section of woods. Do you?"

"No. Never been here before."

Hildy's mind whirled with thoughts of how they could escape. Her eyes were riveted on the leaping flames ahead, so high and hot that Vester stepped back from them. The smell of fire from behind was becoming more intense.

"When Vester mentioned a cave, he motioned to his left," Hildy explained to Ruby. "That means he must know that area of the woods fairly well. But maybe he doesn't know the woods so well in the other direction."

"Then let's try that way!"

The girls took off running to the right while the dry storm exploded around them. Lightning flashes and thunderclaps continued without rain.

Vester, momentarily distracted by the flames, cursed at the girls and yelled, "Ye cain't get away!"

Hildy glanced back. "He's coming after us!"

"Run faster!" Ruby cried.

The girls scrambled up a steep hill, moving at an angle. They stumbled over exposed roots, downed limbs, and tangles of underbrush, falling at one point and tearing their dresses and scuffing their new shoes.

Hildy twisted her head in the direction they'd come. "He's gone!"

Both girls scanned the area from every angle, but their pursuer had vanished.

"Where'd he go?" Ruby asked, her voice betraying her concern.

"I'm more worried about the way that wildfire is building," Hildy said. She squinted through heavy smoke that poured from a growing corridor of flames to their right and left. She added, "Soon's we get a little farther ahead, we can cut back to our right and go down the hill. We'll have outrun the fire he set."

Ruby shook her head. "We cain't outrun the one the lightnin' set! It's a-spreadin' every which way, faster'n anything!"

The girls began running again, hearing the fire crackle and roar as it rapidly spread out of control.

Suddenly, Ruby pointed and skidded to a stop. "Yonder's Vester! See him? He done cut across an' got ahead o' us!"

Hildy's eyes darted about, seeking safety, but there was none. "Can't go that way!" she exclaimed. "We've got to go back the way we came!"

"But the flames!" Ruby's voice was high with fear. "Lookee! Them on top o' the hill's comin' down fast, jumpin' from tree to tree! An' the one Vester set's a-comin' up the mountain jist a-whoopin' an' a-hollerin'!"

"We've got no choice! We'll run right between them and get back past the fire Vester set! We can run around its end and down to the church where it's safe!"

The girls ran back the way they'd come. By now, smoke from both fires was heavy and added to the gloom of the skies. Hildy silently prayed for a heavy rain to douse the two fires. The sky flickered with countless lightning flashes followed by the booming thunder that echoed through the mountains.

After a while Ruby glanced back and announced that she couldn't see Vester. "Maybe the fahr done cut him off!" she added hopefully.

Hildy's anxious eyes probed ahead as they topped another mountain ridge. Then her heart lurched and sank. "Look!"

She pointed at the two lines of fire. They were roaring toward each other, leaping from tree to tree and threatening to join up on the side of the next mountain.

Ruby cried in despair, "Them two fahrs is a-gonna meet afore we kin get 'round the end and down to where it's safe."

Hildy swallowed hard, her blue eyes searching around for another way out of their worsening situation.

One glance up the mountain showed that lightning had struck at least two more trees. Flames and smoke curled up in widely separated places, but close enough to the original strike to show they would quickly meet and form one solid wall of fire.

Hildy spun around to look back. The black sky seemed to leap with dancing flames. For a moment she wondered if Vester had been caught in the fire, but she had to pay attention to their own situation.

"Oh, Hildy!" Ruby wailed, "What'll we do now?"

"There's an open space covered with rocks at the bottom of this hill!" She pointed. "See it?"

"Yeah, but what good'll that do?"

"Maybe it's big enough that the fire'll burn past us! Anyway, it's our only chance!"

Hildy ran toward the spot, with Ruby one step behind. They reached the bottom of the hill, anxiously scanning the rock outcropping. It wasn't nearly as big as the escarpment where Hildy had sat a few days ago, but it was an oasis of safety that wouldn't burn, while everything else was trees and underbrush.

About fifty yards ahead of them, a white-tailed deer bounded away in panic. Close by, Hildy heard frightened squeaking noises of tiny creatures fleeing for their lives from the advancing blaze. The animals were heedless of the girls near them.

As Hildy and Ruby rounded a corner of the rock outcropping, there came a gruff, startled *woof!* from the dense brush.

Hildy stopped short. "What was that?"

"What was *what*?" Ruby asked, pausing for breath.

"I thought I heard a dog."

"There's no dogs out—" Ruby was cut off at the sound of a large animal crashing through the underbrush to their right.

Hildy gulped and stared, "That sounded like a—a bear!"

"Ain't hardly no bears left in the Ozarks!"

Hildy's heart was beating hard from exertion and fear. She

squinted again toward their destination. "What's that black spot in that cliff ahead?"

Ruby coughed from the smoke and rubbed her eyes before answering, "Maybe it's the cave Vester mentioned!"

"Can't be! He indicated the opposite direction. Anyway, let's go see."

The girls stumbled, nearly exhausted, to the dark spot in the small cliff. "It's not a cave," Hildy observed, "but I think we can squeeze inside and get out of the fire and smoke."

Hildy cautiously peered into the entrance. Beyond, she saw a small, dark space about three feet high and five feet deep. "Phew!" she exclaimed, making a face. "Smells terrible! This must be an animal's den!"

"Is thar an animal in thar?" Ruby shrunk back.

"No. I can see the back wall. I think it's safer in here than it is out there."

The girls entered the den, Hildy in the lead. The space was cool and damp, but the rank stench almost sickened Hildy. At least there was no smell of smoke. The cousins crawled to the back and flopped wearily onto the ground.

"We're gonna be safe here!" Ruby said with a grin.

Hildy was too winded to answer. The thunder and lightning continued unabated, and the forest fire burned furiously beyond their rocky place of shelter.

Suddenly Hildy tensed and cocked her head to listen.

"What'd ye hear?" Ruby asked hoarsely, her throat still scratchy from the smoke.

"Shhh!" Hildy whispered fiercely.

Someone—or something—was approaching the den. Hildy could tell from the sound that it was big.

Ruby asked in a low voice, "Is it Vester?"

A low, gutteral sound rumbled just outside the entrance. The girls scrambled into a tight embrace. Seconds later, a massive head appeared in the opening at the front of the den.

"It's a bear!" Hildy screeched.

—

CHAPTER NINETEEN

TERROR AT THE CLIFF'S EDGE

Hildy froze, her back against the den wall, her eyes on the head of the huge black animal blocking the entrance. Even though bears in the Ozarks had been hunted almost to extinction, the fire had obviously driven this two-hundred-pounder into the open. His rank odor was powerful, making Hildy realize what she'd been smelling since entering the shelter. She and Ruby had stumbled into a bear's den!

Hildy whispered fiercely, "Don't move!"

"We cain't stay here!" Ruby whispered back.

"We can't get by that bear! And even if we did, we'd be right back in the fire!"

The bear stood on all four legs looking into the den and sniffing noisily. Hildy felt goosebumps race up and down her arms. She stared in fearful fascination at the immense forepaws equipped with powerful hooked claws.

Hildy heard Ruby make a little sniffling noise. This made the bear cock his head as though trying to see what strange creatures were in the den's deep shadows.

Hildy leaned over to whisper in Ruby's ear, "Feel around and see if you can find a stick or something."

The bear made an *Uff!* sound and swung his head back and forth.

Ruby cried in a tiny scared voice, "He's comin' in after us!"

Hildy shushed her cousin and felt the ground for some kind of weapon with which to defend themselves. *Maybe the bear's as afraid of us as we are of him!* Hildy thought frantically. *Or maybe he's just trying to escape the fire and won't bother us if we don't bother him!*

Ruby leaned close to whisper in Hildy's right ear, "I didn't find nothin'!"

"Me either," Hildy answered aloud.

The bear let out a startled *Oof!* and backed off a couple of shuffling steps. Then it turned and bounded away in a rolling gait for about twenty feet, only to stop and swing back to face in the direction of the den.

Hildy whispered, "I don't think he can decide whether he's more afraid of us or the fire."

"I jist wish he'd keep a-goin'!"

"Keep your voice down! If this is his den, he won't leave it so easily!"

"I didn't think bears had dens this time o' year."

"From the smell of this place, he's been here recently. And if he thinks it's safer in here than out there in the fire—"

"Don't say it!" Ruby shook her head in horror.

Hildy's eyes were riveted on the bear. He rose to his hind legs and stood upright like a man. He seemed to be as tall as the trees burning behind him.

In a moment, the bear dropped down again on all fours, still facing the opening to the den. They girls were motionless.

Finally, Ruby whispered in a shaking little voice, "I been a-thinkin' about what muh daddy said in his sermon. I come mighty close to hatin' all them people who said such turrible things about me all those years, about not havin' no pa.

"It made me feel powerful good to show him off these last

few days and make 'em see how wrong they was! Makin' 'em
eat crow an' ever'thing." Ruby giggled nervously.

Hildy watched the bear without answering. It had not moved
except to make loud snuffing noises.

Ruby's voice was barely audible. "I don't know as I exactly
hated them folks, but well—ye reckon it was close enough to
make me a liar an' a murderer?"

Hildy wished her cousin would be quiet, but she realized
being this close to death was stirring Ruby's conscience. Hildy
asked softly, "Would you be willing to tell people you're sorry?
To make up with them?"

"I'd do anythin' to get out of this mess, but they ain't nothin'
I can do!"

"You could pray."

"Ye know I ain't no good at such things. But if'n ye wanted
to, that'd be okay with me."

Hildy nodded, her eyes still on the huge wild animal watching them. For a moment, she thought she'd welcome Vester's
appearance to scare the bear away. Then she shuddered. *No, I'd
rather face the bear!* she thought.

"Hildy, are ye a-prayin'?"

"Not yet."

"Tell Him I'm plumb sorry for the way I been a-feelin' about
gettin' even with them folks for what they said and done to me."

"I'll tell Him." Hildy was glad Ruby had come so far this
summer, but her cousin still wasn't ready to speak directly to
the Lord.

Ordinarily, Hildy would have prayed with her eyes shut, but
she kept them glued to the bear and prayed in a barely audible
voice. She asked for help in getting out of their situation, then
raised her voice slightly for Ruby's benefit: "Lord, hear my cousin's words and forgive her."

After the prayer, Hildy lifted her eyes beyond the bear to the
sky. The thunder and lightning seemed to be farther away. She
was vaguely aware that the fire beyond the bear, across the rocky
outcropping, was moving on. It left behind a wide patch of land
where smoke curled up from the hot weeds and brush that had
burned moments before.

"Oh, Lord!" Ruby exclaimed, pointing at the bear.

Hildy wasn't sure if Ruby's outburst was a prayer or a startled exclamation. She watched the animal rise again on its hind legs, sniffing loudly. He backed up a step, began clicking his huge teeth, then dropped back ponderously to all four feet. Then in a rolling, purposeful gait, he waddled toward the den.

"He's a-comin' back!" Ruby cried in a squeaky voice.

The bear growled deeply from his huge chest. He opened his mouth, showing lots of big teeth, and began clicking them again threateningly.

"He's a-gonna get us!" Ruby whispered hoarsely.

Hildy suddenly remembered something she'd read, about bears being frightened away from President Roosevelt's Civilian Conservation Corps camps, where young men did environmental work in California's High Sierras.

Her mouth dry from fear, Hildy explained, "I read that if you bang on pans and yell—"

"We ain't got no pans!" Ruby interrupted, grasping her meaning.

"Then we'll clap our hands and yell! Maybe—"

Before she could finish, Ruby let out a screech that nearly broke Hildy's eardrums. It was her instinctive reaction to Hildy's idea for scaring the bear away.

It seemed to work, because the bear made a startled grunting sound and spun around, half facing away from the entrance.

"He's turning!" Hildy shrieked. "Clap your hands!"

"Shoo!" Ruby cried. "Scat!"

Hildy had heard those words used countless times to scare away a stray cat or chickens, and to hear them now made her laugh in spite of their situation.

The bear started off in a loose, rolling motion that reminded Hildy of two boys in a gunnysack racing at a Fourth of July picnic. The animal went straight for the rocky ground cover and then to the area where the fire had just passed. With barely two steps into the burned area, it let out a squall of pain, and bounded downhill with an angry roar.

"He's gone!" Hildy exclaimed. She scrambled on hands and

knees to where she could peer outside. Raising her eyes, she could see the fire still raged beyond except for one strip of untouched woods.

"Come on!" she cried, jumping up. "Let's run through that stand of trees and circle back to the church!"

The girls made a dash toward their last visible place of escape, in the opposite direction from where the bear had gone.

Ruby said hopefully, "Reckon we skeered that old bear so bad he'll be in the next county by now!"

Just then the dark, glowering skies seemed to open, and the long-awaited rain fell hard.

Ruby yelled, "That'll put the fahr out, I reckon!"

"I sure hope so!" Hildy replied, running as fast as she dared without tripping and falling down the steep mountainside.

In a few minutes, soaking wet, breathing hard, but safe, they approached the edge of the forest. Hildy panted, "Let's stop! My heart's about to burst!"

The cousins paused and looked around. They'd come through the forest and were in an open area. To the left, beyond some high brush, Hildy could see houses and knew that Possum Hollow and safety awaited them. To the right, she recognized the top of the steep sandstone cliffs she'd seen during her recent time away to "think."

In the distance behind them, the forest was still blazing brightly in spite of the heavy rain. But the thunder and lightning were dissipating.

"We're going to make it," Hildy said through labored breath.

Ruby laughed with relief, throwing her face back so that the rain washed it. "Safe! We're safe at—"

"Ha!" A man's voice interrupted Ruby's glad cry.

Vester Hardesty walked out into the open, between the girls and Possum Hollow. His black slouch hat was soaked, and his reddish beard was matted against his pockmarked face.

"So here y'all are!" Vester said, his yellow teeth showing through his beard. "For a spell, I figgered ye was both burned up in that fahr!"

He spread his arms and started moving toward the girls. "I

was plumb desperate to find ye! If'n I didn't, the hex that ol' granny widder put on me woulda done me in for shore!"

Hildy and Ruby clutched one another and stood in the pouring rain, still gasping for breath from their run and now the fearful sight before them.

There was a gleam in Vester's eyes as he approached. "Ain't no sense a-tryin' to get away no more!"

Hildy knew she and Ruby were too exhausted to escape Vester. He was completely at home in these rugged mountains and in far better physical condition than they were. But she instinctively grabbed Ruby's hand to make a break, when she heard a slight movement in the brush behind Vester.

"A bear!" she screeched.

Vester let out a wicked cackle of a laugh. "Cain't fool me with that ol' trick!"

But the bear exploded from the brush with a roar, heading straight for Vester who pivoted to face the raging beast, now charging at his hapless victim and clicking his fearsome teeth.

As Hildy pulled Ruby along, she couldn't help but notice that the bear lifted his feet oddly, as if in pain.

He's been burned, and he's mad! she thought.

The bear roared with pain and anger as it bore down on the unarmed man. Vester turned and ran.

Ruby called after the bear as she would a dog, "Sic him, Mister Bear! Get him!"

Hildy watched with mixed feelings of relief and concern at the almost comical chase. Normally a man could not outrun a bear, but its burned paws apparently kept the bear from reaching full speed as it gingerly maneuvered through the brush and up the hill after Vester, who had begun to scramble up the incline.

Beyond the ridge, Hildy could see the tops of a few scattered trees. She guessed Vester was trying to reach them and climb to safety. But Hildy also remembered that black bears could climb trees as well.

Suddenly she realized where he was headed and let out a yell, "Vester! Stop! Don't go that way! You're running straight toward the top of those cliffs!"

Vester didn't seem to hear, and kept running.

In spite of all he'd done to make her life miserable, Hildy felt sorry for the man. She knew he was heading straight to his death.

As she watched helplessly, Vester topped the small rise and disappeared on the other side, the bear still in pursuit.

"He's done trapped hisself!" Ruby said in disbelief. "If the bear don't get him, he'll go over them cliffs—it's a hun'ert feet straight—!"

Her voice broke as a terrible, hoarse cry drifted back from beyond the trees.

"It's too late!" Hildy said sadly. "He's gone over the edge!"

The two frightened girls stood in their tracks, uncertain of what to do next.

There were no more human sounds, but the bear reappeared over the top of the ridge, growling menacingly.

"Don't move!" Hildy cautioned as she felt Ruby tense to run. "Maybe he won't see us."

The bear passed by, oblivious to the girls' presence below, and disappeared into the brush.

Ruby let out a big sigh of relief. "Come on!" she said with urgency. "Let's get back to the church while we still kin! The fahr's still liable to get us if'n the bear don't!"

Hildy shook her head. "Not yet. We've got to go see about Vester."

"What? Ye heard him yell as he went over the cliff. We'll jist notify the sheriff."

Hildy wished she could accept Ruby's suggestion, but she couldn't. "I've got to go see," she said.

Ruby groaned in disgust and disappointment, but knew she had to follow her cousin. They climbed up the ridge toward the cliffs. Nothing moved on the broad, flat plain. There was no sign of Vester or the bear.

"I feel kinda sorry for him, but—"

"I've got to go closer," Hildy said, pulling Ruby with her.

"What? Ye might fall over too!"

Hildy didn't answer, but eased up to the top of the cliff and carefully looked down.

Through the pelting rain, her eyes skimmed the valley floor far below. There were huge boulders and smaller rock slides, but no evidence of Vester.

"Where could he have—?" Hildy asked as Ruby stopped carefully beside her.

"Ohhh-hhh!" A low moan came from the left of where the girls stood.

"It's Vester!" Hildy gasped.

The heavyset man gripped the protruding root of a tree about three feet below the lip of the cliff. The toes of his heavy boots were barely resting on a small rocky ridge, slick from the rain.

"He'p me!" he called. He had lost his hat, and his hair and beard were wet and matted, his eyes wide with desperation.

For a moment, Hildy stood in shock. Then she dropped to her knees. "Ruby, give me a hand!"

"Why should we he'p him?"

"Ruby, stop being foolish, and help me!"

"They's no way we kin do anythin' for him! He's too heavy!"

"Then run to the church and get help! I'll stay and do what I can!" She reached her right arm over the edge. "Vester, grab hold of my hand!"

Slowly, the man let go of the tree root with his right hand and extended it upward. "I'm—hurt—inside!" he whispered, his voice filled with pain.

"Hildy, he'll pull you over the edge!" Ruby warned.

"Then *help* me!"

Ruby muttered something, but dropped to her knees beside Hildy just as Vester's wet, dirty hand closed over Hildy's wrist. At that instant, the root he was holding with his left hand suddenly gave way.

Hildy was jerked flat onto the slippery ground and dragged face first toward the edge of the cliff!

CHAPTER TWENTY

HEADING HOME

Ruby!" Hildy screamed, desperately extending her free hand toward her cousin.

Ruby dived forward, grabbed Hildy's left arm above the wrist and tugged hard. At the same instant, Vester's weight eased on Hildy's other hand. Her forward slide came to a halt, her shoulders extending just beyond the top of the awesome cliff.

Heart pounding, Hildy scooted backward on the muddy ground until only her face was past the cliff. Vester still looked up at her from his new perch, barely securing the girl's small hand.

"Got me another toe hold jist in time," he explained weakly. "Not shore how long it'll hold—"

"Can you find another root or something to hang on to?" Hildy urged. She turned to Ruby, "Brace yourself and keep me from going over if he slips any more."

"I'm a-tryin', but this ground's gettin' mighty slippery! If he drops again, he'll drag us both over!"

"If I start to slide, you let go! Now, don't talk! Just hang on!" Hildy looked over the edge again. "Vester, did you get another handhold?"

"Found me a bit of a rock ledge. Slicker'n a greased pig, but it's all I kin find."

"How about your feet?"

"Got muh toes stuck in a crack or somethin'."

"Good! Now, put a little weight on them. See if you can lift yourself up. Easy! That's it! Now, while I pull on your hand, move the other one to that piece of broken root."

"I'm a-tryin', but I'm stove up inside."

"Don't think about it! Just reach!"

As the rain continued to wash over Hildy's face, she watched in amazement as the man who had been her enemy obeyed her instructions. "Now," she went on, shaking water from her eyes and mouth, "Move your farthest foot up slowly. See if you can find another foothold."

Gradually, the injured man moved laboriously up to where his hand on Hildy's wrist was just above the cliff top. "Reach up on top now," she said, "and feel around for a sapling. I'll hold on to your other hand. Ruby, don't let your feet slip *now*!"

Without waiting for a response, Hildy continued speaking to Vester, "Got a good grip on that little sapling?" He nodded, and she commanded, "One good pull should get your head above the top. Okay, all together now! Pull!"

With Ruby pulling on Hildy's left arm and Hildy's right tugging on Vester's hand, the man's head slowly rose above the escarpment, followed by his shoulders.

"Keep pulling!" Hildy cried, straining with the effort. "We've got to get his chest onto the ground!"

Suddenly, Ruby let out a frightened cry and started to skid feet first through the mud toward the precipice.

"Let go and save yourself!" Hildy cried.

Instantly, Ruby let go of Hildy's hand and grabbed wildly for the only thing available, the same little tree where Vester had a precarious grip.

It made little muffled popping sounds. Hildy warned, "You're pulling it up by the roots!"

Ruby had stopped her dangerous slide. She let go of the

sapling and pushed herself backward on her stomach, away from the cliff.

"Ruby, get back a little farther, and then hang on to my legs!" Hildy instructed. "Vester, let go of my hand and dig your fingers into the ground—hard! I'll grab your overalls and pull with both hands. Get onto your chest if you can!"

The sapling popped out of the earth in Vester's hand. He dropped it fast and grabbed for the ground. Hildy clutched his overalls and heaved with all her strength, Ruby pulling on Hildy's legs.

Slowly, the man's shoulders rocked forward, then his chest. He fell face downward. Ruby let go of Hildy and rushed up to grab hold of Vester's overall straps with Hildy. Together, puffing and straining, the girls yanked him across the slick muddy ground until his heavy boots were also on solid soil.

Then all three collapsed on top of the cliff.

Hildy smiled weakly. "Thank God! We made it!"

————

Hildy stayed with the moaning, prostrate man while Ruby ran through the storm to bring help. When she returned with several men, the forest fire was almost out, but the rain continued to fall heavily.

Mr. Garvin took Vester in a spring wagon to the nearest doctor at the county seat. Hildy and Ruby, safe, and in dry clothes provided by women of the area, sat again in the small church with their grandmothers, Nate, and Iris.

There they related how they both found themselves deep in the forest when the fire broke out, their encounter with the bear, with Vester, and then the incredible rescue effort.

When they finished telling their tale, everyone was quiet with wonder and gratitude. Nate offered a prayer of thanksgiving for their safety and a request for Vester's recovery.

As Nate said, "Amen," Granny spoke up. "Vester's shore to make it. And I'm a-gonna tell him they ain't no hex on him. Never was. He jist believed there was, and that got him into a peck o' trouble."

Hildy smiled. "Thank you, Granny. Then he'll have no reason to harm you anymore." She paused, then added carefully, "Granny, when Ruby and I came out of the forest with the rescuers, I couldn't help noticing that you and Grandma Skaggs were holding hands. What happened?"

Granny nodded, her dark eyes suddenly soft with a light Hildy had never seem in them before, "Well, you know I shore didn't like what Nate said in his sermon 'bout people bein' liars and murderers jist 'cause they didn't get along with their kin."

"Them's the Lord's words, Granny, not mine!" Nate reminded her.

Granny smiled faintly. "Anyway, Gussie an' me, while we waited, watchin' that fahr—not knowin' if'n ye was dead or alive, well, we agreed that we both was fools. And we finally come to our senses and done what the Good Book tol' us to do."

Ruby's grandmother added, "Hepzibah and me realized that if anything happened to y'all, it would be our fault."

"Gussie's right," Granny added, smiling at her older sister, "The waitin' and not knowin' got to us both, and we each said we was sorry to each other and to God."

"We're both set in our ways," Ruby's grandmother said, "but we've made a start. Why, I even asked Nate here to forgive me for tellin' him to never darken muh door again. And while Hepzibah an' me got some years left, and the good Lord willin', we want to try to live together like when we was girls!"

Granny glanced at Iris, who sat quietly at the end of the pew. "Gussie and me asked Iris if'n she'd come live with us, too. And she said yes."

Hildy softly exclaimed, "Oh, I'm so glad! For all of you!" She walked over to Iris and embraced her.

"You're the best friend I've ever had, Hildy. I'll never forget you. Thank you for all you've done."

"Thank you, Iris. I'm glad I could help."

In all the excitement, Hildy had forgotten about the news that had sent Ruby into the woods in the first place. "Uncle Nate, tell us about your call to preach here."

"Well, the church did ask me to be their reg'lar preacher, but

I told them I couldn't give my answer till after we all get back to Lone River."

Ruby gave a sigh of relief.

"Will you leave tomorrow, Uncle Nate?" Hildy asked.

"Yes, Hildy. Me'n Ruby got to. Ye comin' with us?"

"That depends—" she replied, glancing at her grandmother.

"Like ye said, Hildy Corrigan, ye belong with yore family. I was a-bein' mighty selfish, wantin' ye to stay here with me. So if'n ye'll forgive me—"

Hildy didn't let her finish. She threw her arms around her grandmother and whispered through happy tears, "Of course I forgive you!"

It was the afternoon of the second day on the train heading West before Hildy and Ruby found a quiet time to be alone. The two Farnham children Hildy was hired to care for were napping, and their mother and father wanted some time to talk by themselves. So the cousins sat in a coach seat alone and watched the scenery whiz by the window.

"You know, Ruby, remember what your father said about claiming Matthew 18:19—'If two of you shall agree on earth as touching any thing that they shall ask, it shall be done for them of my Father which is in heaven'? I think that was probably why everything turned out all right in the Ozarks. Now we're almost home again."

Ruby nodded without speaking.

Hildy continued, "And home is wherever Dad and Molly are, with Elizabeth, Martha, Sarah, Iola, and Joey. And Mischief, of course."

"And muh place is with muh daddy, wherever he goes," Ruby agreed, " 'ceptin' on that freight train with that ol' bull Mr. Farnham bought."

"You think your daddy'll accept the call to preach in Possum Hollow?"

"I don't have no idee, but if'n he does, I'm a-gonna go with him. 'Course I'd rather stay in Californy."

"It may be selfish," Hildy said thoughtfully, "but I hope he doesn't. I don't want to be away from you."

"Same goes for me, Hildy. Fact is, I was thinkin' how nice it'll be for us to start school together on Monday."

"I hope we can. But before we left for Arkansas, Daddy said he might get laid off his riding job, and he'd have to go looking for work. But even if he doesn't, we've got to move out of the barn-house."

"Will ye move into a reg'lar house?"

"We can't afford one. More likely to be a tarpaper shack. But someday—someday—" She had to pause before finishing fervently, "no matter what happens, we're going to find our 'forever home' and we won't ever have to move again."

Ruby reached out impulsively and squeezed her cousin's hand. "I know ye will!"

Hildy smiled. "Thanks."

"What about Spud? Reckon ye'll ever see him again?"

"I hope so," Hildy said wistfully. "Maybe there'll be a letter waiting for me when we get home." *Home!* The word gave Hildy a warm, pleasant feeling.

No matter what kind of dangers she had faced in the past, and no matter what kind of troubles were ahead, Hildy was sure things would work out because of the Lord's care, and because she was part of a family that cared about each other.

Secure in her deep and abiding faith in God and in her family, Hildy leaned forward to look out the train window. *It's going to be an exciting year!* she told herself.

The train's whistle sounded sad and lonely, yet pleasant at the same time. Life was like that, and Hildy liked it.

The train rattled on toward the West, carrying the cousins toward a world of new experiences, fresh challenges and high adventures.

ACKNOWLEDGMENTS

The author gratefully acknowledges the help and information received from the following people and organizations: William M. Shepherd, Arkansas Natural Heritage Commission; Keith Sutton, publications director, Arkansas Game and Fish Commission; Jennifer Danley, field interpreter, Arkansas State Parks; Jamie Worth, Ozark National Forest, Buffalo Ranger District; Wallace Keck, Devil's Den State Park; and Neil Compton, M.D. , retired physician active in conservation.

The author is solely responsible for the accuracy of information found in this book where he took minor literary license for dramatic interest.